THE CASE
OF THE
MISSING S.I.P.

Also by H. Lena Jones

Caged: Where Most Husbands Should Be … for a While

Trapped on Planet Liska

THE CASE OF THE MISSING S.I.P.

H. LENA JONES

iUniverse, Inc.
New York Lincoln Shanghai

THE CASE OF THE MISSING S.I.P.

iUniverse, Inc.

iUniverse books may be ordered through booksellers or by contacting:

iUniverse
2021 Pine Lake Road, Suite 100
Lincoln, NE 68512
www.iuniverse.com
1-800-Authors (1-800-288-4677)

This is a work of fiction. All of the characters, names, incidents, organizations, and dialogue as well as [location] in this novel are either the products of the author's imagination or are used fictitiously.

ISBN-13: 978-0-595-41723-0 (pbk)
ISBN-13: 978-0-595-86062-3 (ebk)
ISBN-10: 0-595-41723-X (pbk)
ISBN-10: 0-595-86062-1 (ebk)

Printed in the United States of America

My sincere thanks and appreciation to my dear husband, Cy, for all his editing and constructive feedback in my third and most challenging novel, so far.

Contents

Introduction

Kids everywhere have an imaginary friend with whom they share secrets. Mine is my handed down, well-worn teddy bear. We have great conversations, like when I told him I was going to set up my own detective agency called Mitch Jones, PI. He said, "How's this for punch? Shoestring Detective Agency … Mitch Jones, PI."

When I asked him if he was being sarcastic, he replied, "'Course not! But nothing in your detective bag is what I would call state-of-the-art equipment, is it? It's anybody's guess what other junk will end up in there. Shoestring describes your homemade operation, kiddo, no ifs, ands, or buts about it."

Anyway, you've just gotta read my story and find out more about my amazing friend, Teddy, and the extraordinary case we set out to solve.

Cheerio,

Mitch Jones, P.I.

PS If you would like a free copy of my personal sketch-map, depicting important locations in the Case of the Missing SIP, e-mail me at mitchjones_pi@yahoo.ca

One
First Contact

Click! Click! Click!

Repeatedly jabbing the delete button on the keyboard, made no difference except to the tip of my index finger—it was beginning to feel numb! The mysterious mass had embedded itself with invisible tentacles among the planets of the solar system. There was only one option left—download the information to desktop, exit the internet, break the link. That should rid my computer of the intruding mass ... forever!

I named the saved file *Science Project*-Solar System.

After several deep breaths, I opened the file with renewed confidence.

The solar system looked normal.

Hooray!

Then it happened!

Out popped the unknown mass again, like a champagne cork! The letters Z-O-R-B pulsed from it and then stopped.

I pounded the desk with my fist. "*Zorb*? There's no such planet! Computers are so dumb."

I closed the file and started to drag the desktop icon to the waste basket.

Suddenly the cursor froze and the icon began a series of rapid pulses. The file opened on its own. I was staring at the unknown mass again.

My eyes widened. "Eh? Morse code? This can't be ... it's sending an S.O.S. message."

N-e-e-d h-e-l-p

"Yeah! Right! Not even NASA would believe this! Come on, computer, I don't have all year to do my stupid science project. I already said Zorb is not a planet! Why do you keep adding it to my project?"

Jason!

Of course! My brother must have tampered with my computer. I'll unscrew his stupid head and replace it with a 25-Watt light bulb.

I charged into Jason's bedroom determined to do just that.

"Were you messing with my computer?"

"Get a life, Michelle. What does it say on my door, eh? *Boys Only!* Translation … no skirts allowed. Go back and read the sign. Make an appointment if you want to speak to me … two months from now … I'm fully booked."

"Go chew your cheesy socks, Jason. I'm here now and I demand to know what you've done to my computer, and especially to PowerPoint."

"Short answer? Nothing! Now make like a bee and buzz off."

Jason sprang up and shoved me out.

I stomped back to my computer. Zorb was still emitting its S.O.S. message. PowerPoint was messing up my head, instead of helping with the project.

I flopped onto my chair.

Tomorrow I would just have to tell Mr. Mulligan that my computer's artificial intelligence had spiraled out of control, caused me to have a severe attack of diarrhea—the life threatening sort, and made me spend the entire night perched on the toilet.

Maybe I should fake amnesia!

Moving to New Zealand was not a good idea, for me, that is. Going to a new school was the main reason; science and Mr. Mulligan didn't help.

"Troubles?" asked my teddy bear.

"Yeah! Big time."

I turned off the computer.

Going to school the following morning was like a visit to the dentist. I didn't want to face Mr. Mulligan. I cringed when he stopped beside my desk, waiting for me to hand him my assignment. When I produced nothing, he narrowed his eyes.

"So what's your excuse this time, Jones, eh? Rats? Raccoons? Which marauding, nocturnal rodent devoured your assignment?"

Mr. Mulligan wasted no time launching his attack. His voice grated in my ear. His bony knuckles, pressed against the top of my desk, glowed white. He poked his mouse-like face so close to mine, the lines around his mouth looked like crevices on a glacier. Two stiff, white hairs, curved like horns on a bull, protruded from the inside corners of his nostrils.

"Well? Today—Thursday—I said I wanted all projects handed in. That includes yours. Didn't you understand that?"

"Sorry, sir, but—"

"No excuses, madam." He glowered. "The science exhibition is on Monday. I want to review everyone's entry before then."

My eyes locked onto Mr. Mulligan's nose hairs like heat-seeking missiles.

Go ahead. Launch the attack dared my thoughts. *Yank them out.*

I sat on my hands to avoid a major criminal offence.

As if reading my thoughts, Mr. Mulligan pulled back, wriggled his nose, and cleared his throat.

"Well?" he said.

"I'm having some difficulty with my computer, sir, I—"

"Difficulty? Ai! Here it comes. What difficulty can you have with a project based on naming and arranging the long-established planets in our solar system, eh, Jones?"

None, sir, but if a planet you've never heard of kept popping up on your screen, you would pluck your nose hairs in frustration, was what I wanted to say. However, I held my tongue.

"I'll hand it in tomorrow, sir. I just have a little something to fix."

"Did you hear that, class? Our little genius will hand in her project tomorrow because she has a little *something* to fix. Better late than never, I suppose. Knowing you, I won't be holding my breath though, Jones."

Mr. Mulligan stomped back to his desk, huffing and puffing like a steam engine.

"Know what, Jones? I don't understand what's in that space between your ears. By all accounts, it can't be much. From what I've been hearing, your Math and English are also in jeopardy. You'd better return to Earth, child. Here is where it's at. Hard work now, pays dividends later. Maybe you'd prefer picking apples for a living."

Those are your thoughts, sir. I may not be an A student, but one day, I'm gonna be the world's greatest female detective. Just watch me.

That night, after tea, the science project took top priority. I was diligent in naming the nine planets and felt confident that the intruding mass would be gone. But the result was the same—Zorb kept reappearing on my computer screen as the tenth planet.

"I already said there are only nine planets, you stupid computer ... and Zorb isn't one of them!"

I slapped the side of the monitor so hard my hand stung. Tears pricked the back of my eyes. Whoever designed the software for PowerPoint must have been drunk, or as thick as the hairs up Mr. Mulligan's nostrils.

"This assignment sucks. Sorry Mr. Mulligan. No submission from me. I suppose I'll be picking apples for a living."

I was beginning to feel like Dr. Marvel—the loony retired scientist who lived on Moa Lane. I had named the nine known planets, shown the sun and all the celestial bodies orbiting it, even included some satellites, asteroids, comets, and meteorites. What was left? Cosmic dust and gases? Should I go overboard and include the Big Dipper? Orion? Or even this stupid Zorb thing? Well, science never was my best subject.

Maybe there was something wrong with my eyeballs.

I jabbed the off switch on my computer. Curling up in bed with a detective novel was far more appealing than science homework.

After changing into my flannel pajamas and sliding under the bedcovers, I reached for the *Hardy Boys* book beside my reading lamp. That's when I noticed another book propped against the base of the lamp—*Sojourners in a World Not Our Own.*

I flipped open the front cover.

"This isn't a library book. It's not even my book. Where did it come from? It must be Jason's."

Older brothers are such a pain!

Jason should have known better than to come into my room, especially since he didn't allow me into his.

"You must read the first chapter," someone spoke.

The voice sounded distant, muffled, and eerie.

Darn Jason! Now he's hiding in my closet, pretending to be a ventriloquist. He must have slipped into my room while I was brushing my teeth.

"Read the first chapter now."

"GET out of my closet, bonehead!" I said between clenched teeth.

I expected the doors to swing open, and my older brother's dark-brown mop of curls to pop out. When nothing happened, I sprang out of bed, staggering between scattered clothes, books, and shoes, and flung the closet doors open.

"OUT, Jason! Now!"

"What's up with you, Michelle?" I heard Jason shout from his bedroom across the hall.

I froze.

Darn that stupid science project! It had finally driven me insane. Now I was hearing voices!

"Reeeead the first chapter …"

The voice, more urgent now, wasn't coming from my closet at all. It was coming from the book!

Impossible! I shook my head. Overactive imagination!

The book began to vibrate in my hand; the voice spoke again.

"Reeeead …"

Icy fingers of fear took a firm grip of my senses. Goose bumps spread like measles over my skin. My throat clogged up.

Don't be stupid Michelle. Books don't talk. You've been doing too much science homework tonight. Your brain's addled.

With as much calm as I could muster, I tried to put the book down, but it seemed to be stuck to my fingers. My left hand moved of its own accord and flipped the book open to the first chapter. My eyes locked onto the words.

> **War has broken out on planet Zorb. I am Boraz, leader of the scientific community of Endar. The rebel Saja and his evil army are closing in on my colleague, Arkon, and me. I fear that our minds will be neutralized, if we are caught.**

Planet Zorb? I should have guessed. Jason must have messed with the PowerPoint software, and somehow concealed a heat-sensitive, micro-voice chip in the book. Instant relief replaced all traces of fear, now. I shook the book, but nothing fell out. I wanted to confront my brother there and then, but curiosity made me read on.

> **Our province, Endar, is rich in mineral deposits and intellectual resources. For decades, Saja and his rebels have been fighting us in the hope of capturing both.**

> **The situation has never been more desperate. Saja and his rebels have already destroyed most of our scientific records, technical equipment, and energy sources. We must find a way to stop him; otherwise our civilization will be lost.**

> **Arkon and I are the most senior scientists left in our province. Our top-secret S1M1 unit contains, for safekeeping, the minds of our**

intelligent people, most of whom have been captured and enslaved. Saja will not be satisfied until he can control their minds—and ours. The S1M1 unit must not fall into his hands. We must escape and reprogram the unit before he can find us.

"S1M1 unit?" I whispered. "Is it a robot, like R2-D2? I must find out." I read on ...

Rajol, my brother, and what remains of our army, will be left to defend Endar from the rebels until we return. Once Saja is defeated, our people will be free again. There are two on planet Earth who can help us—one is young; she must find the other.

Wow! I wanted to read on, to find out if I was right about the S1M1 unit being a robot, but my drooping eyelids dictated otherwise.

Still clutching the book, I began drifting in and out of sleep. My radio emitted static noises then went silent altogether. But I didn't remember turning it on, in the first place. An eerie quietness filled my room. I began to hear muffled voices, and I could see shadowy forms, but I wasn't awake. I was either hallucinating or having a weird dream!

"That's her!"

"How can you be so sure?"

"Look at her ... the only difference is, she's asleep. Besides, observe the book she's holding. It's the one we projected ..."

"Should we wake her and tell her about her assignment?"

"No. We don't want to frighten her. Look at us ... we haven't assumed human form yet."

"But we have no choice. Our time is short."

"We must switch to telepathic communication."

A cool breeze caressed my face. I could see that a blue, hazy light had illuminated my bedroom. Was I awake or still dreaming!

I sensed I was not alone, yet I felt no fear.

"Hi, detective," said someone.

The voice sounded in my mind.

"Who's there?" I heard myself say, though my lips didn't move.

"Detective Jones, it is I."

"Detective Jones?"

"My father is in the next room—opposite the toilet."

The blue light shifted a bit. Two ghostly forms materialized.

"No, it's you we want, detective Mitch Jones." One spoke.

"My name's Michelle, not Mitch. I'm not a detective. You've got the wrong person."

The form shimmered. "We have not made a mistake. We must speak with you. You're a wanna-be detective, aren't you? You've got detective paraphernalia in your detective bag, haven't you?"

This one must be the leader. He was doing most of the talking.

"Okay, don't blow a gasket. What do you want from me?"

"You have to help us. We're from planet Zorb. I'm Boraz and this is Arkon."

"Planet Zorb? Boraz? Arkon? Hey, you're fictional characters in a Sci-fi book I was reading. Plus I've been spending too much time on my science project, that's why I'm having this crazy dream."

"This is not a dream, Michelle, or Sci-fi as you call it. As leader of the people of Endar, I command you to listen without interrupting.

"Zorb is near the outermost reaches of the solar system—it is a planet that is yet to be discovered by your Earth scientists. We tried to make initial contact with you through your science project, but you ignored us. We are real. We are desperate for your help, so listen well.

"As you have already read, Saja, the rebel leader, is after us. He wants the S1M1 unit. By now, he knows we're on Earth and any time soon, he may arrive, if he hasn't already. While we're in our alien state, he can track us down. To avoid this we must hide. We must occupy human bodies."

He sounded real, but I was still convinced I was having one heck of a nightmare.

"You want to occupy *my* body? Why not take my brother's?"

"No, Michelle, we don't need to occupy *your* body. We just want your help."

"You want me to help you *find* a body ... two bodies?"

"Not that either. We want you to help us reprogram our S1M1 unit."

"Heard of that Lucas movie-making guy? He knows lots about robots—"

"No, we need you."

"Why me? How am *I* supposed to help you? With your superior intelligence, what use is a twelve-year-old Earth kid?"

"We chose you because you have an inquisitive mind and a determined spirit."

"That might be so, but I can't help you because you're fictional—not real."

"Oh, please, not that again! Look, we are from outer space, and we need your help."

"Okay, okay, so you're real. What help can I offer you?"

Funny how dreams can fool you!

"The S1M1 unit must be reprogrammed in case Saja finds it. Once the reprogramming is completed, Saja cannot access the stored data or alter the minds it holds."

"So this Saja person is ruthless, and your S1M1 gadget, which contains your peoples' minds, is vulnerable. Somehow I'm supposed to help protect these minds by reprogramming your unit. Hey, something's wrong with this picture. I'm not Luke Skywalker or Princess Leah or—"

Just then, one of Dad's loudest snores blasted through my bedroom wall, sending my startled visitors crashing into each other.

"Sorry, Michelle." Boraz shimmered away from Arkon. "That thunderous explosion exposes our vulnerability in this present state. We must go now. We've found a safe hiding place in a huge concrete storehouse across Wellington harbor. It is called ... Te Papa."

"New Zealand's national museum? But you can't occupy that place. You'll get into trouble. You'll get handed over to the authorities and they'll use you for specimens—you know, alien life forms—extra-terrestrials! You'll be dissected like frogs, and your S1M1 unit will become scrap."

Boraz was uninterested in my feeble attempts to explain the consequences.

"Many people guard the exhibits at that place," he continued. "Some have protruding chests and buttocks, others do not. We prefer the shapes with flat chests and narrow buttocks. They would be much easier to balance. We will borrow two of those types of bodies."

"However, once we have occupied the bodies of those flat-chested, narrow-bottomed human specimens, we will be unable to continue our work," said Arkon. "That's why we need your help. But you'll need the help of one other."

Arkon's voice faded and his form shimmered.

The blue light surrounding the intruders flickered as if a gentle breeze had disturbed it. Boraz and Arkon began to fade.

"We ... must ... go. You find ... other," said one of the almost invisible forms.

"Wait! Who is this *other*? How will I find him or her? How will I find you?"

"The book ... only way ... to communicate ... with us." Both spoke in unison, strengthening the volume.

"But who is this other? At least tell me that."

"Energy depleted … you … must … find … other."

"Help … us. Help … with … S1M1."

"Is it a robot, like R2-D2?" I asked.

The blue light flickered one last time, before extinguishing.

I snapped out of my daze, muttering incoherent words.

Realizing I was lying on my back with my mouth wide open—a position which often caused me to have strange dreams—I flipped onto my side and drifted back to sleep.

In the morning, I awoke feeling exhausted. It was 8:00AM. Time to get ready for school.

Disjointed memories of my dream stampeded across my mind—aliens hiding at Te Papa, and them telling me to find "other".

"Boy, Michelle," I whispered. "You sure have some wild dreams. You'd better learn how to control that overactive imagination of yours."

"Maybe God is preparing you for something unusual," said Teddy in my mind.

"Yeah, right, Teddy. Thanks for nothing."

I forced myself out of bed.

I checked the Sci-fi book again for Jason's hidden chip. There was none.

"My brother thinks he's so smart. He must have sneaked into my room, while I slept, and removed it. I've a good mind to smear glue on his guitar strings."

I jabbed the power button on the computer and pulled up my project. Nine normal planets stared at me.

Thank heavens!

But just as I was about to save to disc, the tenth planet popped onto the screen, pulsing like a beacon.

In a flash, the planets changed into lopsided shapes. The word ZORB zigzagged across the screen, leaving in its wake, a scrawled message, pulsing one letter at a time. *B-o-r-a-z … r-e-m-e-m-b-e-r … f-i-n-d … o-t-h-e-r!*

Two
Dr. Marvel

I handed in my project with reluctance. Mr. Mulligan's black beady eyes locked onto mine like giant magnets. I couldn't even blink.

"No lame excuses? No assignment-eating rodents? I didn't believe you had anything to hand in, Jones." His temple veins pulsed, so did the nose hairs.

"Sorry to disappoint you, sir. But just wait 'til you see it."

Mr. Mulligan narrowed his bushy eyebrows. "You haven't included Martians, have you?"

"Let's just say something extraordinary included itself, sir—something I can't explain just yet."

Huffing and puffing like a steam engine, Mr. Mulligan stormed off to his desk, slapping the side of his leg with my assignment. He began his lecture with the benefits of following instructions and earning high grades. But I was busy thinking about the name Boraz, and the words flashing across my computer screen. What did "find other" mean?

Okay, Jason, I thought, *it's time to stop this nonsense. I'll unscrew your head and attach it to your keyboard for tormenting me like this. You will regret tampering with my computer and leaving that weird book in my room. Just you wait!*

"Will someone shake Jones out of her daze," I heard Mr. Mulligan shout.

As I rode home from school that breezy Friday afternoon, I hoped Dad didn't have any urgent detective business over the weekend, because that would spoil our Saturday tramping expedition over the Days Bay ridge track. I loved to study the cabbage trees and silver ferns which are unique to New Zealand. Then on Sunday afternoon, we would drive to the Southward Car Museum. I liked to look at the old cars. Al Capone's was my favorite.

BOOM!
BANG!
WHOOSH!

I braked hard, bringing my bike to a dead stop as another Whoosh sailed over my head.

Firecrackers!

Why would anyone be setting off firecrackers in the middle of a sunny afternoon in April? That's when I realized I had stopped right in front of Dr. Marvel's house.

I was just about to jump on my bike again when his front door burst open and he came staggering down the steps, his hair frazzled and standing on end, his face smudged, and his wire-rimmed glasses dangling from one ear. Suction cups with hose-like extensions bobbed from his forehead.

"Hi Dr. M, what's going on?"

I waved, but as soon as he saw me, he spun around like a top, and sprinted back up the steps, leaving a faint trail of smoke seeping from the seat of his pants. I had seen Dr. Marvel in a state of panic several times, but this was the first time I had seen his backside on fire.

Everyone knew Dr. Marvel was retired, though he, himself, seemed unaware of that fact. He believed life-forms existed on other planets, and was always working on some new invention to prove it. No one was surprised whenever fire engines screamed up to his house.

Dr. Marvel would be about six feet long if you stretched him out, but at seventy, old age stooped his lean frame. His gray hair was always unkempt. His bushy moustache drooped at the ends. Most times, he wore a white lab-coat, but today he had on a pair of old gray pants and a long-sleeved, navy sweater.

He lived alone at #35 Moa Lane. No one knew whether he was ever married or had any children or other relatives. His house was on the opposite side of the valley from ours. Numerous shrubs and trees lay between our house and his, but it was possible to get there by tramping through the bush, taking care to avoid the occasional wild rose bramble and our neighbor's noisy German Shepherd.

One evening, not long after we first moved to Days Bay, Dr. Marvel invited us to his house for 'tea'. "Must look after my Canadian friends, ya hear." His Texan accent was cute.

To us Canadians, tea meant just that—a cup of tea with cookies, or cake—so we had eaten a meal beforehand. To our surprise, Dr. Marvel had set the table for dinner, though all the utensils were mismatched.

He seated us before asking whether we preferred seafood, poultry, or red meat. We chose seafood. We didn't want to tell him we had already eaten, since he had gone to so much trouble.

Dr. Marvel retreated to the kitchen, and after a few minutes returned with five opened cans of sardines. He plunked one on each of our plates. Yep! He expected us to eat the sardines straight from the aluminum cans.

I wondered what he would have served if we had chosen poultry or meat—raw chicken or a live sheep, perhaps?

"Ah, seafood! It's good for the heart," he drawled, taking his seat at the head of the table. "Enjoy. Shall we say grace … in silence?"

We bowed our heads.

The rank smell of sardines filled the room, making my stomach queasy. I kept sniffing and had to fight the urge to cover my nose. My brother, Jason, had difficulty restraining his giggles, and so had to keep clearing his throat. Dr. Marvel offered him cough medicine.

Mom came to the rescue and asked Dr. Marvel if he had any lemons. He fetched three half-squeezed soggy pieces from the fridge. Mom cut off the green fuzzy bits before squeezing a few drops onto my sardines.

Dear Lord, I prayed, *don't let me suffer from scurvy after this.*

Somehow, we survived the main course. When Dr. Marvel asked if we would like mousse for dessert, we declined with one voice, fearing he may serve us canned moose meat or, worse yet, a live mouse!

By the time we left Dr. Marvel's house we had learned a few Kiwi expressions. 'tea' meant 'dinner', 'your shout' meant it was your turn to buy the drinks, and "bring a plate" did not mean an empty plate—it should have something edible on it.

I was almost home now. An overhanging Karaka branch nearly swiped me off my bike. The sight of a shiny, silver Toyota Camry parked in front of our garage stirred my curiosity. I braked hard, skidding to a stop alongside the unfamiliar vehicle. One door of our garage was open. Dad's gray Land Rover was there.

"Not a new client please, Dad. You promised you would be free this weekend," I muttered.

Three
The Man from Te Papa

After dumping my bike in the garage, I slunk back to the Camry, peering inside for telltale signs of ownership—gender, occupation, and personal attributes.

Except for a short computer cable lying on the rear seat, there was nothing to indicate ownership. Had someone stolen a computer? What an insult to my dad's intelligence if he had to investigate a minor theft. Maybe the stolen computer contained volatile data like people's private records. Maybe the owner was a doctor!

My curiosity soared.

I galloped up the steps to our glossy red front door. I turned the knob and opened the door quietly. I eased myself into the hallway like a cat burglar.

Dad's office was in the flat below our living room; the door at the top of the stairs was ajar.

I could hear voices.

Eavesdropping was Dad's pet peeve, but I flattened my body onto the carpet, and positioned my ear close to the gap.

Trying not to breathe too deeply, I could just about hear the interview.

"Bodies don't just evaporate into thin air. You do realize this is going to be quite a challenging case to solve, don't you, Mr. Ihaka?" said Dad. His voice was gentle but firm.

Evaporating bodies? That got my attention! The client wasn't a doctor. He must be a mortician and had lost some bodies from the morgue!

Invisible magnets pinned me to the floor.

The man coughed. "Yes, detective, that's why I've s-come to you. Your reputation to solve impossible s-cases s-preceded you all the way from s-Canada

… the great white s-north, the land where the s-Mounties … er … the red-coats on horseback … always get their s-members."

His voice was raspy plus he had a pretty bad lisp or something.

Dad cleared his throat. "Indeed, the Canadian Mounted Police do always get their man."

"s-Precisely what I said. You're s-quick on the drawers."

"Draw—" Dad drummed his fingers.

"See what I s-mean?"

"He's full of baloney," I whispered.

This Mr. Ihaka sounded like a twit who needed a new set of dentures. I whipped out my detective notebook from my backpack and scribbled: *Twit. Full of baloney. Problems pronouncing following words: cases, north, Mounties, members, precisely, quick. (Speech impediment may be due to loose-fitting dentures!)*

Mr. Ihaka cleared his throat. "As I was saying, Mr. Jones, it's hard to believe something of this s-magnitude s-could've happened at s-Te s-Papa. Our museum is tightly secured," he said.

Whoa, I thought, *Te Papa?* Dead bodies aren't kept there, only a few papier-mâché statues. My thoughts went into overdrive as elements of my dream flooded my mind. The aliens Boraz and Arkon had said they would occupy two human bodies at Te Papa.

Come on Michelle, get real, I thought. *It's just coincidence Dad's client is from Te Papa. You dreamt about aliens because you read about them just before going to bed. Your overactive imagination is working overtime.*

Mr. Ihaka's raspy voice jarred me back to the present.

"The SIP, and whoever stole it, s-must be found as soon as s-possible. It's crew-shall."

"That's C-R-U-C-I-A-L," Dad spelled.

"No, it's S-I-P, that's capital S … s-capital I … s-capital P," corrected Mr. Ihaka.

Silence—a long one!

I was anxious for Dad's client to continue because I wanted to know what had happened at the museum and what or who was capital S, capital I, capital P; and how many bodies had been evaporated! Something else tugged at my detective instincts—the tone of Mr. Ihaka's voice. It kept changing as if he had two personalities, like Jekyll and Hyde.

What was the word for that? Schizo—something!

"Have you kept any evidence? Like the guard's cap or baton?" asked Dad.

"Yes, both are in s-my locker at s-Te s-Papa."

"I'll need to check them for finger prints, you understand," said Dad.

Mr. Ihaka coughed and cleared his throat again. "Yes, of course, Mr. Jones. Can you come now?" he said without lisping. "It would be a good time because ... er ... because ..."

"Come on, come on, sss-spit it out," I whispered, growing impatient.

"Well s-can you, detective?"

"Hmmm," said Dad. "I'll have to wait for my kids to come home from school, before I'm able to."

Schizophrenic! That's the word. It described Dad's weird client. Helping Dad solve this new case was just what I needed to stifle my crazy alien dream.

A sudden tickle in my nose made me sneeze.

Blast!

Carpet fluff!

"Michelle?" Dad called out.

Double blast!

"Michelle?"

"Yes Dad. Just came in."

"Is Jason up there?"

"No, Dad. Bet he's over at Brian's."

I heard Dad jabbing the touchtone buttons on the telephone.

After a short pause, he said, "Hello Mrs. Janssen, Alwyn Jones, here. Is Jason there? Er ... yes ... could you ... tell him to come home ... yep, right away. Thank you ... bye. Now Mr. Ihaka, I'll be at the museum within the hour."

Two sets of footsteps pounded up the stairs.

I scrambled to my feet and braced my back against the wall. The thought of seeing Mr. Ihaka face to face made my pulse race.

He was a heavyset man with a broad face—Maori, for sure, but I could be wrong because there were no visible tribal markings. He was about five and a half feet tall. A bushy gray moustache hid his top lip and stretched a full inch either side of his wide nose. His straight, gray hair lay flat on his head. He would be about sixty. He wore a loose-fitting black suit and a white button-up shirt, but no tie. He looked normal—I had no idea what a schizo person should look like.

Mr. Ihaka hobbled past me; hesitated and turned his head. He narrowed his eyes and licked his lips.

"S-curiosity s-kills the s-cat, little girl." He tapped the side of his nose with a crooked index finger.

No doubt, the digit was a reflection of the man.

His breath, a mixture of tobacco mingled with coffee, almost knocked me over.

I wrinkled my nose. "It's *kills*, not *skills*, and *cat*, not *scat*. Curiosity kills the cat." I barely moved my lips or dared to inhale.

Mr. Ihaka glared at me with hard, expressive eyes.

"That's what I said. See that *you* remember, s-'cause you don't want to end up like the s-cat."

Okay, I'd dismiss the schizo thing. Maybe it really was just his dentures. I could understand that, but something about his eyes made me feel uneasy. In my book, everyone was a suspect, particularly those with glary eyes and changing speech patterns. We detectives could never be too cautious.

I would have asked him about the computer cable in his car, but I didn't want him flinging the 'curiosity' thing at me again.

From the front door, I watched as he and Dad marched along the concrete path towards the steps leading down to the garage. Something about the way Mr. Ihaka hobbled made me even more uneasy. It was as if he had some difficulty with his shoes, or maybe his body was just too heavy for his short legs. Perhaps he needed to lose some weight … or wear bigger shoes!

Mr. Ihaka said something to Dad, spraying him with spit.

Dad pulled out his handkerchief and wiped his face.

"Yuk! Stinky s-s-s-spit!" I whispered, wiping my face with the back of my hand.

I was still staring hard at Mr. Ihaka, when he turned and glared at me. His large, dark eyeballs seemed to spit fiery darts. I pulled back involuntarily. A shiver raced up and down my spine with bone-tingling urgency. This was not good.

I was glad when Dad trotted back to the house.

Four
Keep Your Nose Out, Michelle

Interrogating your own dad is tricky business, but I had to do it.

"So what happened at Te Papa, Dad?"

I waited, notebook and pencil poised ready, like an eager news reporter.

"Were you eavesdropping, Michelle?"

"The door was ajar. So who was murdered at the museum?"

"What have I told you about eavesdropping?"

Dad's eyes bulged. His narrow face, so much like mine, turned blotchy red.

"But, Dad, if I'm to help you solve this case, I need information," I protested, waving my notebook like a flag. "You've taken me on stakeouts before. You always let me help; said it was good experience. So, who stole what, got murdered, and how many bodies were there?"

Dad ran his fingers through his dark-brown wavy hair. "Put the notebook away, Michelle. Listen! This is for your own good. For the record, this case is not about a murder, okay? I can't tell you anything else about what happened at Te Papa because it's confidential. The less you know the better. I'm sorry, Fifi. I *don't* want you involved. I *don't* want you anywhere near this case. And I *don't* want you pestering me for details about it. Understand?"

Fifi! I didn't like that nickname. It was fine when I was a kid. Now it made me feel like a dog wanting its ear scratched. I slouched, my head drooped, and my bottom lip protruded. My hands sweated from the tight grip I kept on my notebook and pencil.

"Fifiiiii!" Dad tickled the back of my ear. "The lip makes no difference. I'm sorry. Believe me … it's for your own good that you should keep out of this case."

"Yes Dad."

"Ah, here comes Jason. Now promise you'll stay put until I get back. Okay?" He lifted my chin. "Look at me, honey."

My best sad puppy-dog eyes stared up at Dad. Maybe I should tell him about the aliens in my dream.

"Promise!" he insisted.

Behind my back, I crossed my fingers, dropping my pencil in the process. "I promise." It was a half-hearted reply.

"That's my girl." Dad kissed my forehead.

"You need to wash your face, Dad. That man sprayed stinky spit on it."

"Michelle! Oh, you're a pest!"

Dad marched off to the washroom, returning within minutes.

"All scrubbed up. Happy now?"

I nodded. "Smells much better, and makes your face look pink and healthy, too."

"That's a relief. Have you any homework to do?"

"Sorta … science … aliens …"

"Good, get on with it. The sooner it's done, the more free time you'll have over the weekend."

"It's Friday. Are we having pizza for tea? Mom would like that."

Dad laughed. "You bet. Mom will be late—important meeting with her colleagues. Have to go."

He kissed me again, before bounding down the steps. Dad never dressed up when he worked. He lived in blue jeans and bulky sweaters. If I were a detective, I would probably wear blue jeans, too.

"No anchovies," I yelled, racing after him. "And no chilli peppers!"

I stood with my arms dangling over the railing, watching his taillights disappear around the corner.

"We need a drummer, Michelle," Jason called from the garage. He and his friends were setting up to make a racket.

"Tie jam-jar lids to your knee caps, why don't you!"

Boys have no imagination!

Jason and his friends liked to practice their rock music. They thought one day they'd become famous! I, on the other hand, wanted to become a private investigator like my father. Imagine that! You would think I would have preferred being with girls my own age doing girly things, like hanging out at the mall and talking about boys, or wasting precious time chatting on the Internet. No, not me, I'd rather spend my spare time doing detective stuff—meaningful stuff like—Te Papa!

From what I had overheard, someone had stolen something called the "SIP". Mr. Ihaka had said he found a security guard's baton and cap on the floor; bodies were missing, but no one was killed. That didn't add up. However, Dad had said no one was murdered and I had to believe him. Why jump to conclusions? After all, I had only heard a small part of the interview.

Memories of my alien dream returned. They were going to occupy two human bodies. What if it wasn't a dream? What if—? Of course it was a dream. I shouldn't have read Jason's silly Sci-fi book!

My right eye began to twitch. That meant something was going to happen, and soon. Only trouble was I couldn't remember whether a right eye twitch was good and a left eye twitch was bad, or vice versa. I always got them mixed up. Either way, something was going to happen.

Five
Mitch Jones P.I.

I needed to think. My room was the only place for that.

Flinging myself across the bed, I landed eyeball to eyeball with my little brown teddy bear.

Teddy's sightless, beady eyes bored into mine.

"What are you staring at, blind bat?" I asked.

"You … where's the old spark?" said the bear. "Where's the old Michelle Jones? Private Eye Michelle Jones? Eagle eye, Michelle Jones—need I say more?"

"What do *you* know? You're only a stupid stuffed animal."

"Am I?"

"Of course you are." I poked his belly. "See, you don't even flinch. Teddy, did anything unusual happen in my room last night?"

"Unusual? What kind of unusual?"

"Did you see anything weird?"

"See? You just called me a blind bat, and now you ask—"

"Well did anything strange happen?"

"Let me think. Yeah, you were talking in your sleep."

"I was? What did I say?"

"Mumbo jumbo, as usual. Why? What did you think you said? Was it something exciting?"

"That's what I'm trying to figure out, Teddy. When I do, I'll tell you. Okay?"

"Some Private Eye you'll turn out to be."

"My eye's twitching."

"Which one?"

"Right."

"Oh, that's baaaaad. You need a plan of action."

Yep! I was talking to a stuffed bear, pretending it was talking back to me, but this was how I focused and stabilized my thoughts, and obtained answers. I hugged Teddy, apologizing for poking him.

If I were determined to be a girl detective, I would have to start by not being offended by Dad's decision to withhold critical information from me and barring me from working on the Te Papa case. I would have to dig for my own clues because this case intrigued me.

A thought sprang into my head.

"Know what, Teddy? I'm going to start my own detective agency."

"Hooray! So you won't be picking apples as a profession?"

Scurrying over to my closet, I pulled out my detective bag. I checked to make sure Dad's old camera, binoculars, and discarded business-card holder, plus Mom's green facemask, my magnifying glass, notebook, pencils, and Groucho Marx's spectacles were all there.

I turned and looked in the mirror. Staring back at me was a slim twelve-year-old with wavy shoulder-length hair, a narrow face, and a thin, straight nose. That girl was me!

"This won't do," said the girl in the mirror. "First you have to change your name."

"Why?" I replied.

"Look it, a top-notch detective gotta have a top-notch name. Try Maud Jones?"

"You gotta be joking. Sounds like a name you'd give to a stubborn old donkey."

Her: "Okay. Try Jonesy Jones, Private Eye."

Me: "Corny. Got any better ideas?"

Her: "Try Mitch Jones. Detective Mitch Jones has a nice ring."

"Eh? Detective Mitch Jones?" The hairs at the back of my neck stood at attention.

That's what the aliens in my dream had called me. Coincidence?

"Mitch—a boy's name—yeah, I like it," I said.

I was doing it again—talking to myself. Nevertheless, I felt compelled to continue.

"Mitch Jones, Private Eye. Mitch Jones, PI Hmmm. Yes, I rather like that. Now what I need are my own business cards, and a badge."

"Hang on PI," said Teddy, in my head.

"What now?"

"How's this for punch. *Shoestring Detective Agency … Mitch Jones, PI.*"

"Shoestring? Teddy, are you being sarcastic?"

"No … but nothing in your detective bag is what I would call state-of-the-art equipment, is it? It's anybody's guess what other junk will end up in there. Shoestring describes your homemade operation, kiddo, no ifs, ands, or buts about it."

"Gimme a sec to think about that, Teddy. Okay, you win, polyester brain. Shoestring Detective Agency it is."

Feeling more positive, I raced to my computer. I opened up Publisher and began to create my own personalized business cards. Pleased with the result, I typed what would appear on my nametag.

Shoestring Detective Agency

Mitch Jones P.I.

As an afterthought, I scrolled through Clip Art and found an old running shoe with its shoelace undone.

"Perfect Logo!" I whispered, plugging and resizing the artwork to fit just left of the word 'Shoestring'.

I didn't have perforated business card paper on which to print my cards, so I used two sheets of pale blue paper instead. After cutting the sheets into twenty individual cards, I stuffed them into my new-to-me business card holder.

Next, I needed to try on my detective gear. Slipping off my blue jeans and sweater, I hauled on Jason's handed-down black tracksuit. The waist was a little slack; I would need a large safety pin. I slipped the tracksuit top on, over my sweater; it was a snug fit. I didn't have black socks, so I borrowed Dad's, folding the extra bit under my toes.

Footwear was next. White running shoes? No, the white running shoes just didn't cut it. I went in search of some black shoe polish, and found a liquid version in the cupboard under the kitchen sink. Soon, I was wearing *black* running shoes. Mom would be mad, but I hoped she would understand once I explained about my detective agency.

I stared into the mirror again and decided to braid my hair into a tight ponytail. It hurt a little, but I wanted to create a slick look.

Another glance at the full-length mirror drew a nod of approval from my reflection. We were both pleased. The girl in black with the serious face, staring back at me was Mitch Jones, PI. Even the new nametag—black print against the light blue background of the paper—looked impressive.

With some reluctance, I changed back into my regular clothes, stuffing my detective ones into my bag. As an afterthought, I retrieved my new nametag, pinning it on my sweater.

I plopped on my bed wondering what else I could be doing to pass some time when I heard a distinct "ping" coming from my computer. I stared at the lit screen. A series of asterisks danced across it forming the words N*eed help!*

Jason! He must have snuck back to his room just to bug me for not agreeing to be their drummer. Somehow, he had rigged our computers so he could send me stupid messages.

I raced to the keyboard and typed: *Listen moron. U need more than help. U need a psychiatrist.*

Another message appeared with rapid strokes:

Not the kind of help required. Need you. Urgent!

As I said before, I'm not available. In your lingo, that's no can do, dude. Ask one of your brainy mates to double as drummer and guitar player, why don't you? P.S. Don't bother replying. I'm really, really not interested! Over and out, moron!

I charged out of my room, hoping to catch my brother red-handed, but when I opened his bedroom door, he wasn't there and his computer was not on. I rushed back to my room. To my surprise, my computer had turned itself off.

"This can't be." I gazed at the blank monitor.

I could hear my heart thumping. Icy fingers of fear jabbed at me, backing me up against my bed. My left heel clipped the end of my night table, sending something tumbling to the floor with a loud bang.

It was Jason's weird book!

I picked it up and shook it hard in case Jason had returned the chip. Nothing fell out. I stared at the picture on the cover; a shiny spacecraft pursued by another. Below them was a round sphere—Earth!

"After last night's dream, I refuse to read you anymore," I whispered.

"We need to talk about the S1M1 unit, Mitch, PI."

The voice spooked me, and the book flew out of my hand as if it had wings. How could book characters be audible? My mind blanked out, but my legs had sense enough to bolt for the nearest exit. I pelted down the hallway as if trying to escape a hungry pack of pit bulls, or a swarm of angry wasps who wanted a share of my butt.

The telephone jingled just before I crashed through the front door.

Leave it, I thought. *But it could be Dad or Mr. Ihaka!*

Six
G. Grimm

I grabbed the receiver. "Mitch Jones … nobody's here … leave clues, if you want … this is a recording—"

"Mitch? Michelle, what's going on? You're breathless."

I gulped. "Mom! Hi! Sorry about my confused state … ran for the phone."

"I can tell that, dear, but why have you changed your name?"

"Er … no reason, Mom. I'm still a girl."

"Thank goodness for small mercies. Are you rushing off someplace looking for clues?"

"Me? Oh no … not really … maybe. Why?"

"Honey, are you sure you're all right?"

"Yeah, Mom, quite sure … couldn't be better … or worse."

"Listen, honey—"

"I'm all ears."

Mom asked whether Dad was home. I told her he was on an important assignment at Te Papa and that he had promised to bring pizza for dinner.

"What time will you be home, Mom?"

"Not later than nine. Keep my share warm, will you, sweetheart?"

"Sure, Mom. 'Bye."

I charged out the front door.

It was almost 4:30. It would be dark soon. My brother and his mates were discussing their music when I popped into the garage.

"Jason, were you tampering with my computer?"

"No. What's wrong with it?"

"Did you leave your book in my room?"

"Nope."

"Have you been here for the past fifteen minutes?"

"Yes. What's with the inquisition, Sherlock?"

Maybe I was over-reacting. Maybe it had been my school pals, Robert and Reuben Owen, playing stupid games with their computer. Sometimes they sent emails with dumb attachments, except the messages on my monitor were not emails; they'd just appeared. My mind was in turmoil. How did that spooky book appear in my room? I would never touch it again—that's for sure.

"Got a virus on your computer, Meechelle?" asked Jason's pal, doing shoulder lifts with two ten-pound apple bags.

"Yeah, Briiiiaaan, that might be it."

"Well, did you plug it in?" asked Brian, pressing the apple bags over his head, a grimace on his face.

I rolled my eyes. "Jason, can I ride my bike down to the waterfront, please?" *Sea air might help exorcise my latest spooky encounter,* I thought.

Jason frowned and pinned me with a 'what's-eating-you, Michelle,' stare. He always knew when something was bothering me. He didn't press further. Instead, he rolled my bike out of the garage.

"Thanks."

He squinted at my badge and laughed. "See that you get back here in half an hour, Mitch Jones, P dot I dot."

"Yeah, okay. Oi, Brian," I said, "you best put real apples or rocks in those empty bags, if you hope to build your puny muscles."

"Say what?" replied Brian, looking confused. "What's she on about, Jason? Don't these bags say ten pounds on them?"

I took off down the road, intending to zip past Dr. Marvel's house at #35 Moa Lane, just to see if he had set himself on fire again. Instead, my bike seemed to take control and I found myself racing down Moa Road. I didn't see the man in a yellow tracksuit jogging across the road, until it was too late. I slammed on my brakes, but the next moment I was sailing over the handlebars, right at him.

For a brief moment we lay there, staring at each other—me sprawled on top of him. I picked myself up just as the man raised his arms to shove me off. He scrambled to his feet.

He was a balding man in his late-fifties, about medium height. He had graying hair and a hawkish face with deep-set, dark eyes.

"Why don't you stupid kids look where you're going, eh?" he snarled, baring a set of yellow irregular teeth.

"I'm sorry," I began, but he stormed up his driveway.

I checked my bike for damage; the man stopped at his front door and stared back at me. Maybe he was concerned about my bike, or me, or both.

"We're okay," I shouted. "Good thing we landed on soft turf."

The man scampered into the house and slammed the door. Why had he looked so nervous? What was he hiding?

I glanced at the letterbox to see who he was. G. Grimm. #35—in gold lettering was painted just below the mail slot.

"Grimm by name, grim by nature," I whispered.

My ride was over. I jumped on my bike and tried to pedal, but the chain slipped off the back sprocket. I pushed the bike home, thinking about the Grimm incident. Peculiar people often have something to hide. I would have to make an entry in my detective notebook.

My thoughts soon returned to what had happened at Te Papa. If I hoped to find clues about the robbery, that's where I needed to be.

The SIP could be anywhere by now—Masterton? Palmerston North? Auckland? Who knows!

Seven
A Strange Phone Call

"Back already, P dot I dot?" Jason raised one eyebrow.

"Yep! Thanks for caring ... the chain slipped off. Please fix it, Jase. Thanks."

I dumped my bike in the garage and raced up the steps. Just as I entered the front door, Dad's office telephone rang. I raced down to the office, but the door was locked. I could only hear snippets of the voice message—a man saying something about Te Papa and midnight. (Dad didn't like the silent recordings. This way he could hear the message before he intercepted the call.)

As soon as the message ended, I rushed to my parents' bedroom and picked up the office extension. I dialed *69. Instead of a ring, there was a continuous beep. Darn! The last-number redial system only worked in Canada and the U.S.

If I could find out the telephone number and name of the caller, I could call him and say I was Dad's secretary. Yeah! Telecom should be able to help. My heart raced at the prospect. I rushed to the house phone and dialed the operator.

I asked my question.

"I'm sorry. We can't give out that information. Don't you have an answering machine?"

"Yes."

"Then whoever called must have left a message. Have you checked?"

"Yes—no ... what I mean is ... they didn't leave a message."

"If it's important, they'll call back." She hung up.

Another dead-end!

A locked office door separated me from learning valuable information about Dad's case. I would have to employ all the tricks in the book to squeeze any information out of him.

I returned to my room. The scary Sci-fi book was still on the floor, but I did not pick it up. I had to focus only on Dad's case. Sitting on the edge of my bed with my detective notebook propped on my knees, I recorded my accident outside 35 Moa Road.

Friday, 4:30PM approx ... Collision
Suspicious man ... Grimm ... 35 Moa Road
Dressed in yellow tracksuit and white running shoes
Caucasian ... Mid-fifties ... Medium height ... Irregular teeth

I snapped my book shut and let my thoughts return to Te Papa and how I should go about investigating the robbery without Dad's knowledge. That's when I saw the impossibility of it. Even if I took the long bus-ride around the harbor to the museum, who would want to talk to a kid? I couldn't just go up to Mr. Ihaka and tell him I knew all about the case because my Dad and I were partners. That would be a lie and would make Dad furious when he found out. Besides, Mr. Ihaka would only spew that "curiosity cat" thing at me, again.

Being a solo detective wasn't easy.

Salty tears stung my eyes. I rubbed them with the backs of my hands.

I needed to focus.

"Hey, PI, it's me."

"What do you want, Teddy?"

"What's with the tears?"

"What tears?"

"The salty liquid that's stinging your eyeballs as we speak ..."

"I'm a lousy solo detective."

"Nah. You've only been a detective for a couple of hours."

"I'm working on an important case, and I don't know how I'm going to question possible suspects?"

"Case, already? Possible suspects, already?"

"Like the man I almost ran over with my bike ... like Mr. Ihaka. There is something suspicious about him, you know. I just don't trust him."

"Ihaka? Head of Te Papa Security Ihaka? You're joking, right? I thought he was your Dad's client. Besides, you have no right jumping to such conclusions about the man, or sticking your nose where you're not supposed to."

"Yes, but … well, I don't know why I said that. It's just a feeling."

"I should watch that if I were you, PI"

Eight
Can't Get Blood from a Stone

At eight-thirty keys jingled at the front door.

Jason and I raced down the hallway, just as the door opened.

Mouth-watering aroma of pizza filled the air.

"Hi, Dad! Yum! That smells good," I said.

I flung my arms around his waist, a ploy I often used to soft-soap him into answering questions—the robbery at Te Papa type of questions.

"Hello, hello, hello!" Dad lifted the two pizza boxes above my head. "Feeding time at the zoo?"

He handed the boxes to Jason.

Dad kicked off his shoes on the mat and stuffed his feet into his house slippers, before following Jason and me into the kitchen.

"Mom's not home yet?" he asked heading towards the kitchen sink.

"Said nine-ish," I replied, reaching into the cupboard for some plates.

Dad washed and dried his hands; then helped himself to two slices of pizza. He zapped his in the microwave.

Jason and I preferred ours lukewarm.

From the Rimu dining table we could look across Wellington harbor to Seatoun. Tonight, the lights were bright and twinkled like stars. Dad and I chatted about everything, except *the case*; Jason gobbled down his pizza. After a few loud burps, he scampered off to his room.

Dad looked tired. He'd had a long day, but I was dying to learn what he'd found out at Te Papa. It was getting late. I had to quiz him now, before Mom came home.

"Found out anything at Te Papa, Dad?"

The direct approach was best.

"What did I tell you before?"

"Nothing. That's why I'm asking."

"I gotta say this, Fifi, you never give up. But there's nothing to tell."

"Can't you tell me just a little teensy-weensy bit?" I gestured with my thumb and index finger. "Pleeeease!"

"You are determined, Michelle—Mitch, P dot I dot?"

"PI, Dad. I prefer it with the periods."

His eyebrow arched; he stared at my nametag. Then he burst out laughing; the tired lines on his face melted.

"Shoestring Detective Agency? Now that's original!"

He folded his arms across his chest.

"Well Mitch PI, I'm sorry, but this time I really, really can't tell you anything. This case is off limits. It's c-o-n-f-i-d-e-n-t-i-a-l." He spelled the word slowly.

Dad pushed his empty plate over to me.

"You're a mean daddy."

"It's for your own good."

I almost blurted out details about my dream, the Sci-fi book, and my computer monitor, but that would have been stupid. Dad would have laughed and made fun about my overactive imagination.

"Did you notice anything a bit odd about Mr. Ihaka, Dad—like Jekyll and Hyde odd?"

He rolled his eyes upwards and folded his arms across his chest. "Give it a rest, eh?"

That was it; end of story! I was on my own. No information—closed book! Can't-get-blood-from-a-stone closed.

I huffed and stamped one foot.

Dad shrugged his shoulders and mouthed "Sorry, final word."

I stamped the other foot; Dad raised one eyebrow.

"Someone left a message on your office phone, Dad."

He shot out of his chair like a cannon ball and raced down to his office. I wanted to follow, but Teddy was yapping away inside my head again.

"Hang tight, Mitch PI, all is not lost. There is more than one way to skin an unsuspecting pussycat."

I cleared the table.

Dad returned.

He flopped into an armchair, and began flipping pages of the Evening Post newspaper.

"I hope you're not going to be tied up all weekend, are you, Dad?"

"Looks like it, I'm afraid." He glanced over the top of the paper. "Duty calls."

He folded the paper in half and tossed it to the floor.

"But, Dad, what about the bush walk? The car museum? You promised."

"Sorry, Fifi. This case is hot. We'll have to do it another time. Have you started your homework?"

"Not yet, I ..."

"Get started."

Dad yawned and closed his eyes.

By the time I'd finished stacking the dishwasher, Dad was snoring. I kissed his cheek and tiptoed off to my room, still fretting about my ruined weekend and failed attempts to get information from Dad. There was no way I could focus on school work, even if I tried.

I was still awake when I heard Mom come home, but I didn't bother to get out of bed. I could hear her and Dad chatting and laughing.

I switched to my private world.

"Hey, Teddy, what did you mean about more than one way to skin a cat?'"

"We'll talk about it tomorrow. I'm sleepy."

"You're stuffed. You can't sleep."

"Watch me."

"Look it, Teddy, you don't sleep. You don't even blink. You just sit there, day and night, staring into nothingness with your beady glass eyes. So what did you mean?"

When Teddy didn't answer, I grabbed his leg and swung him around a few times. He remained silent.

"Say something, dummy," I demanded, holding him upside down.

"Snore!"

I stuffed him under a spare pillow, buried my head under mine, and begged my thoughts to be still. I must have drifted off to sleep because something jolted me awake.

Talking!

Dad was talking, but not to Mom.

He was on the office extension; the piercing ring had woken me.

I tiptoed into the hallway and sneaked towards my parents' bedroom door. Even one side of a telephone conversation was meaningful to a good detective!

I pressed my ear to the door, just in time to hear Dad say, "Yes, that's an ideal location for it … I'll have a look."

Ideal location for what? I wondered.

The receiver clicked; I heard Dad moving about.

"Now, where are you going?" said Mom.

"Won't be long. I just need to walk off the pizza."

"Want company?" said Mom.

"Nah! You've had a long day, honey. Get some sleep. It's past eleven."

Dad hardly ever refused Mom's company. Something was up. I'm sure it had to do with that phone call.

When his footsteps moved towards the bedroom door, I scooted back to my room. I changed with haste into my black detective clothes. This way, I could follow Dad, without being seen. Time did not allow me to put on my black running shoes, so I plunged my feet into my bedroom slippers.

I heard the front door open and close, and waited until Dad had walked past the front gate before I slipped out after him.

I shivered and wrapped my arms around my body. I should have hauled on my windbreaker. Sharp stones poking through the bottoms of my soft-soled footwear made following Dad much slower.

Dad walked at a steady pace. He turned up Moa Lane. When he reached Dr. Marvel's driveway, he stopped to look at the house on the opposite side of the road.

Dad had only gone a few steps past Dr. Marvel's when I noticed a bright red beam of light, the thickness of a straw, shoot out of Dr. Marvel's chimney. I followed its upward arc until it disappeared into the night sky. I wondered what that was about!

I turned my attention to Dad. He had reached the end of the lane and stood looking around. Was he waiting for someone, or something?

Suddenly someone in a long, black raincoat stepped from behind a leafy bush. My heart missed a beat. I clapped my hand over my mouth, stifling a warning shout. Dad turned and walked toward the person, as if expecting them.

From where I stood, only the person's back was visible under the dim streetlight. I noted the shoulder length hair pulled back in a loose ponytail. Dad and the person talked for a short while, before Dad fished something white from his pocket; an envelope, perhaps.

"What's Dad up to now? Rendezvousing with a woman at this time of night?" I whispered. "No wonder he didn't want Mom tagging along."

The stranger shoved the envelope into a pocket, before melting into the darkness.

Dad began a slow walk home.

I ducked behind a large cluster of Agapanthus, holding my breath as he marched past. I counted to twenty to give him a good head start. When I peeked from behind the bush, he had stopped and was staring again at the house opposite Dr. Marvel's.

Why was he interested in that particular house?

When he moved on, I waited a few more minutes before emerging from my hiding place. As I passed the house, I paused to see what Dad had found so interesting.

The house was in darkness, as if the owners were out for the evening. A floodlight illuminated a group of cabbage trees on one side of the driveway.

Nothing was unusual about that!

Dad had rounded the corner now. I increased my pace. Just as I made it round the bend, he was skipping up our front steps. I slowed down to give him enough time to get indoors and into bed.

When I reached the front door, I made a horrible discovery. I was locked out! There was a spare key in the garage, but I needed the remote to open the garage door. Even if I got the spare key, it would be of no use because Dad would have engaged the safety chain inside our front door.

I slumped onto the doormat and cradled my head; my right eye twitched madly.

"Dad's going to crucify me when he finds me out here," I whispered, fighting back tears. "And Mom's going to crucify him when she finds out about that woman."

"Try your bedroom window," came Teddy's muffled voice in my head.

I scrambled to my feet and raced to my bedroom window. It was ajar, but only just. I reached up and pulled it out some more, enough for me to squeeze through. There was only one problem. It was too high. It wouldn't be easy to pull myself up. I needed something to stand on.

Think, Mitch, think.

The rubbish bin flashed in my mind.

I tiptoed to get it from the back porch. It was full of smelly rubbish and was too heavy to carry. I dumped the individual bags onto the porch, and plopped the lid on top of them. Then, I carried the empty rubbish bin to my window and positioned it upside down. I managed to climb through the window, but my feet kicked the bin over, just as I tumbled head first onto the bedroom floor.

"Did you hear that bang?" I heard Dad say.

"More like a thud. Must be possums scrounging around for food," Mom answered. "At least the rubbish is secure."

"Saved your behind, but not your bacon," mocked Teddy.

I felt around the bed for him. "Where have you got to now?"

"You buried me, remember?"

I reached under the spare pillow and dragged him out. "Sorry."

"Your voice sounds funny. What's up?"

"Got more problems, Teddy," I whispered.

"Such as?"

"I just saw Dad with a woman."

"A woman? Yeah, right. Get real, Michelle. Your pops wouldn't notice even if one stood naked in front of him with bells on her navel."

"Maybe you're right, Teddy."

"Ain't no maybe about it, detective."

But I still had another problem to think about—possums! If they attacked the rubbish in the night, how would I explain the separation between rubbish bags and bin? I'd worry about that tomorrow. I kicked off my slippers, and gave the bottoms of my feet a quick rub, before hauling on my PJ's.

Sleep was not forthcoming even though I tried counting sheep, chickens, and even possums. It's a curse being a detective's daughter! Frustrated, I switched on my bedside lamp. My eyes locked onto the Sci-fi book that was still on the floor. I stared at the picture, almost daring the two spacecraft to move. Like a zombie, I climbed out of bed and picked it up.

"This time don't drop it," said a voice, barely audible.

I gasped, but tried not to panic.

"Who are you? Are you a ghost? Don't you know you're dead?" I whispered bravely.

"It's Boraz. You must find the other!"

I froze.

The sound of Dad flushing the toilet jolted me out of my stupor. Once again, the book plummeted to the floor with a thud.

"Michelle? Are you still up? What was that noise?"

Dad's tapping on my bedroom door broke my paralysis.

I sprang into bed. "I … I was reading, Dad, and the book fell. Goodnight."

I left the lamp on and pulled the bedcovers over my head. I wished for sleep to come, but it refused. The talking book, my computer monitor, Mr. Ihaka, memories of Dad and his midnight rendezvous, kept marching through my head. Was I beginning to lose my marbles, like Dr. Marvel?

"Sleep, what's keeping you?" I yawned.

"Empty your mind of thoughts," said Teddy.

Nine
Another Way to Skin a Cat

Jason strumming his stupid guitar and singing at the top of his voice about rubbish and possums woke me. It was nine o'clock. Sunlight streamed through the window.

I jumped out of bed, kicking something against the wall.

The Sci-fi book!

I ignored it.

I dashed to find my parents, but they had already left—Dad detecting and Mom at the university. When I went to the bathroom, there were two messages stuck on the mirror.

Mitch, honey, could you stick the white towels in the washing machine. No bleach, just a hot wash. Thanks, Mom.

I read the other message. *Michelle, clean up the mess, Dad.*

"So you've seen the messages, detective," said Jason, leaning against bathroom door, a wide grin across his chops. "You'd better go detect which possum separated the rubbish from the bin, P dot I dot."

"Ha! Ha!" I shoved him aside and raced to the back porch.

The plastic rubbish bags were in shreds; rubbish scattered everywhere. Damn those possums! They were not so cute anymore and I was ready to volunteer my services to capture them for winter coats.

I grabbed Mom's old rubber gloves. Holding my breath, I began the clean-up process with haste.

I showered right after.

All through breakfast, my thoughts lingered on the mysterious woman Dad had spoken to on Moa Lane. But what if it she were a he? Could he be the man who had phoned and left the message about Te Papa on Dad's phone?

Why did Dad have to meet him in the dead of night? Why couldn't he have come to Dad's office like everyone else?

I remembered what Teddy had said about there being more than one way to skin a cat. What had he meant?

That's when an idea popped into my head and my mood brightened.

"Thank you, Teddy."

I raced to my room and switched on my little radio. My dopey brother would think I was still in there. I grabbed my notebook, and sneaked out again, pulling the door shut behind me. I knew how to obtain the information I needed.

I pressed my ear against Jason's bedroom door. He was busy tapping away on his keyboard. With him glued to his computer—and that could be for hours—I was free to do my detecting.

I snuck into my parents' bedroom. I knew Dad hid a skeleton key in his underwear drawer—only I wasn't supposed to know.

My fingers sort for and found the key in question.

Two keys were on the ring—one large, one small.

What I was about to do was wrong, but Dad had left me no other option.

Soon I was standing outside Dad's office door. I planted the skeleton key into the lock and turned it before I could stop myself.

I eased into the office and crept up to Dad's large Rimu desk. Somewhere in one of those two locked file drawers was his pocket-size tape recorder on which he stored his interviews. I gave each drawer a gentle tug. To my surprise, they opened. How careless of Dad!

I combed through two drawers of file folders, boxes, and books, but there was no tape-recorder.

"Come on, Dad, where did you … ah ha, the pencil drawer! The recorder is small enough to fit in it."

It was the only locked drawer! I didn't have a key to his desk … or did I?

My fingers shook slightly as I aimed the skeleton key towards the lock. Before it even connected, I realized it wouldn't fit in the tiny keyhole.

"Well, if that's where the tape-recorder is, I'll just have to break in," I whispered.

I uncoiled a paperclip and, with shaking fingers, aimed it at the lock. It was a slow process, but with persistence, there was a click at last. I pulled the drawer open inch by inch. For a few minutes, I stared at the tape-recorder. I knew what I had to do, but my arms felt like lead. This was dishonest. This was disobeying my father. This was—!

"Get on with it, for Pete's sake," said Teddy in my head. "You don't have all day."

I jumped up and pushed the office door shut so Jason wouldn't hear anything. My heart thumped. I raced back to the desk and plopped into Dad's swivel chair. I picked up the recorder and pressed the rewind button, just a little at first.

I pressed the play button.

No voices!

Only the whirring sound of spinning wheels!

"Darn!"

I depressed another button and the little door on top of the recorder popped open.

No cassette!

My eyes darted about for Dad's stash of mini-cassette tapes. I reached towards the back of the drawer and my fingers collided with a metal box. I pulled it forward. Rows of tiny cassettes, all neatly labeled, stared up at me.

"Bingo!"

Now I needed to locate the right cassette. I glided my index finger across the tops of the cassettes, while my eyes scanned the labels.

"Come on, Dad. Where did you put it?"

Sweat formed across my top lip. I leaned back in the chair and tried to calm myself. Maybe he took it with him. Nah. He wouldn't do that.

Breaking into my dad's desk had been a waste of time and would earn me a month of hard labor, with ball-and-chain, or worse—solitary confinement! I shoved the recorder back into the pencil drawer.

"Some hot-shot chicken detective I am," I muttered, heading out of the office.

"Yo!" Teddy's voice halted me mid-stride. "Have a look under the mug marked *coffee*."

"Huh?"

"Which part of what I said didn't you understand? Coffee or mug?"

Deciding not to continue arguing with myself, I raced back to Dad's desk and lifted the coffee mug.

There it was!

The mini cassette!

My eyes widened.

Te Papa—Ihaka, printed in bold letters were staring at me.

"You are marvelous, Teddy."

"Ain't that the truth!"

Okay, so I was doing it again—talking to myself! But I had found the object of my quest.

I plopped into Dad's chair. With renewed anticipation, I retrieved the recorder, slotted the tiny cassette into place, and pressed the rewind button for a short time, before pressing the play button.

At last—Dad's voice! I turned the volume down and held the recorder to my ear.

"Have you kept any evidence …"

I'd heard that part before, so I pressed the rewind button again, holding it down a bit longer this time.

"It's hard to believe something like this could have happened at s–Te s–Papa …"

I'd heard that part too. I rewound the tape much further this time, before pressing the play button.

"Interview with Mr. Harry Ihaka, Head of Security at Te Papa. 3:20 p.m. Friday, 16 April 1999."

Bingo!

This was it!

I pressed the stop button.

I was at the beginning of the interview, but now I wasn't sure I wanted to go through with it. My heart hammered against my chest wall.

Suddenly, I was shaking all over.

I have to do this for you Dad. You need my help, I know you do.

Jason's footsteps tramping across the hallway towards the door to the flat made me jump. Gas bubbles rolled around in my tummy—baked beans for breakfast was not a good idea!

"Michelle," he yelled. "Where are you?"

The upstairs telephone rang.…

Ten
The Interview

Phew!

When I heard Jason say "Hi Brian!" the bubbles escaped, sounding like air from a deflating balloon.

Instant relief—on both counts!

Jason and his friend could talk for ages! He would soon forget he was even looking for me.

"Get it over with, Mitch PI, either you want the info, or you don't." Teddy's voice echoed again in my head.

"This is wrong. It's like stealing—stealing is wrong."

"You want to help your pops or not?"

"Yes, you know I do. But what if he comes home?"

"Just get on with it."

Taking a deep breath, I opened my notebook—pencil poised ready—and pressed the start button.

"Dad, I'm only doing this for you, because I want to help."

"How can I help you, Mr. Ihaka?" said Dad's voice from the tape recorder.

"Well Mr. Jones, I have a s-major s-crisis on s-my hands. There has been a robbery at s-Te Papa, and I s-need you to investigate it, right away. It's top s-priority."

"A robbery? What was taken?"

"The SIP."

"And what exactly is … er … a SIP, Mr. Ihaka?"

"Not just a SIP, Mr. Jones, it's THE SIP. It's a highly s-confidential s-piece of s-pie."

"Spy?"

"S-machine, detective, I s-call it a s-piece of s-pie so outsiders won't s-know what I'm talking about. Get s-my drift?"

"Not really. Wait, I get it. You call it a piece of pie. Okay, I'll bite. What is it exactly?" Dad cleared his throat.

"Er … the SIP is a s-top-secret device, s-containing information that is of vital importance to, umm, s-national security. It arrived yesterday. I s-took delivery of it s-myself and had it stored in a safe s-place, among some special exhibits, thinking it would blend in and s-not cause any s-curiosity. I instructed Frank, one of s-my best security guards, to be watchful over those particular exhibits. I didn't s-tell him anything about the SIP. What he didn't s-know s-couldn't hurt him. I left s-Te s-Papa at six for—ummm—home."

"And when do you think the robbery occurred, Mr. Ihaka?"

"That's what I don't s-know. When I returned to work this morning, the SIP was not among the exhibits. Frank's baton and s-cap were lying on the floor. It had s-to have happened sometime after I left—but before I arrived for work at eight this morning."

"What about this Frank? Have you questioned him?"

Mr. Ihaka coughed and spluttered. "S-now there's another s-puzzle. I s-can't find him. Ummm, that worries me."

"You're saying an important piece of equipment has gone missing, and so has the security guard?" I heard Dad's fingers tapping on his desk—something he does when his brain needed to work fast. "Have you tried phoning him?"

"Yes, both at home and on his cell-phone … only got a recording."

"No-one just disappears into thin air. Were there any signs of forced entry? Anything at all?"

"S-none."

"Were any other security guards on duty last night?"

"Yes, but I s-couldn't s-question them, s-could I?"

"Did anyone else know about the SIP?"

Mr. Ihaka coughed for a good ten seconds before he spoke again.

"Except for s-me … er … s-no-one s-knows anything about it. You are the … er … first s-person to s-know, and you s-must s-keep it to yourself."

"Have you contacted the police, Mr. Ihaka?"

"Ummm, no, that is out of the s-question. I don't want any s-publicity, you understand. That's why I've s-come to you, Mr. Jones, in s-private."

"How would you describe this machine exactly?"

"Let's just say it looks something like a laptop s-computer, but it's not really."

"Well, either it is a laptop or it isn't, Mr. Ihaka. And, by the way, you never did say what capital S, capital I, capital P, stands for?"

"It's an acronym for … I'd better write it down; then I'll have to destroy the s-paper."

I could hear faint scratching sounds.

"Here. This is what it s-means."

"I see … and this concerns your … hang on, you just ate the paper!"

"Best way to destroy s-top secret information. Once you find the SIP, Mr. Jones, I intend to s-move it to, ummm, s-Papa s-Two s-Toes, for safekeeping."

"Spapa Stoo Stows? Where's that."

Mr. Ihaka cleared his throat.

"Begging your s-pardon, Mr. Jones, that's where I'm from."

"Is that someplace here in New Zealand?"

"Yes … yes, of s-course."

"Hmmm. Can't say I've heard of the place, then again, I don't know all of New Zealand yet."

After a short pause, Dad spoke again.

"Bodies don't just evaporate into thin air. You do realize this is going to be quite a challenging case to solve—"

Although I had already heard the next part of the interview, I continued listening. By the time the interview finished, I had made three pages of notes. I didn't record the interview word for word, just the key points.

Whatever SIP meant, it had to be important to make Mr. Ihaka eat the paper he had written on. Now I see why Dad didn't want me involved.

Although there was nothing in the interview to explain what the SIP did, I had heard enough to tell me it was powerful. According to Mr. Ihaka, it looked like a laptop computer, but it wasn't. I suspected that whoever stole the SIP must have thought it was valuable and might try to sell it to a computer shop, or even try to hack into it.

Satisfied the recording was at the exact spot where Dad had ended the interview; I removed the cassette and returned it to its hiding place under the coffee mug. I replaced the tape recorder in the pencil drawer, wondering how I could lock it. Dad was bound to suspect I had broken in. I would have to worry about that when the time came.

Now I had one last bit of detecting to do—listen to the telephone message, which I overheard, the day before.

I rewound the answering machine and played the messages until I recognized the man's voice. The message was brief.

I know who did the Te Papa thing. Information costs money. Moa Lane at midnight.

That was all. I scribbled that in my notebook too; then pressed the fast-forward button. The burring sound of the tape rewinding, triggered images in my mind of Dad's midnight meeting with the person in the black raincoat.

It wasn't a woman!

Dad must already know who stole the SIP. Or did he?

I noticed a scratch pad next to the phone.

"This must be what Mr. Ihaka wrote on," I whispered, tilting the pad towards the light.

I could see a faint impression of letters. Picking up my pencil, I shaded in each letter with light strokes. The words *Superior Intelligence Protector* emerged. So, that's what SIP meant!

I tried to fit the pieces of the puzzle together. The Superior Intelligence Protector was of vital importance, according to Mr. Ihaka; but why? Neither the Maori people nor New Zealand was under terrorist threat. This wasn't making any sense, but I wrote the new information into my notebook.

I felt satisfied, but guilt ridden. I just hoped Dad didn't need a pencil from his desk drawer for a day or two, at least. In the meantime, I had some deep thinking to do. A machine called the SIP had been stolen. A security guard named Frank had disappeared. Was there a connection? Was Frank the culprit? But according to Mr. Ihaka, Frank knew nothing about the SIP. I ruled him out as a possible suspect, for now.

Thoughts of the aliens in my dream burst into my mind. What if *they* were real? What if *they* were the perpetrators of the Te Papa crime? What if—?

"You've already decided to dismiss this as a trick of the mind, Michelle," I whispered, "a dream is a dream—nothing more, nothing less."

Eleven
Scientists under Suspicion

I replaced Dad's spare keys in his sock drawer. Guilt gnawed at my conscience. I had to find a diversion, a book on artificial intelligence, or something. I rummaged through the bookcase.

Gone with the Wind; War and Peace; Sherlock Holmes Mysteries; Body Language; Mythology! Woooooh! I ran my fingers back. *Body Language!*

I flipped the book open and read the first thing I saw.

Arms folded across the chest suggests a closed mind. If you're talking to someone who suddenly folds their arms, it indicates that they're no longer interested in what you're saying. I flipped to another page.

Handshakes. A firm grasp of the hand indicates genuineness; a limp grasp of the hand indicates insincerity.

I flipped to another page. *What the eyes indicate. Eyes are the windows to the soul. Shifty eyes indicate an insincere person. Honest eyes will look directly into the eyes of the other person.*

A picture of Dad hung above the bookcase. I didn't dare look at it.

I grabbed Volume One of *Sherlock Holmes* and flopped into an armchair. I was halfway through the first chapter of *The Dancing Men*, when the telephone rang.

It was Robert, one of the Owen twins. They were almost a year my junior.

"Doing anything important this morning, Michelle? Wanna go for a bike ride to Pencarrow lighthouse with us?"

"Ah … no … not really … yes … no … I don't think so."

Robert laughed. "What's the matter with you? You kinda sound funny. Are you in trouble?"

"Yeah … ah … no … got a lot on my mind, I guess."

"Wanna talk about it?"

"Not really … well, yes, maybe."

"Boy, Michelle, you *are* weird this morning. Would you like my brother and me to come over?"

"What about your ride?"

"Mom and Dad won't mind. See you in five."

I hung up. "That was so stupid," I scolded myself. "I can't discuss Dad's case. Te Papa and the SIP are confidential. It wouldn't be right to involve the twins. I suppose I could swear them to secrecy and hope for the best. Besides, I might need their help, plus I need to know about those silly computer messages."

Jason's computer still held him hostage. He did not hear the twins arrive.

Both boys were wearing identical blue jeans and red sweaters. Telling them apart was difficult for most people, but I had them sorted. Robert's eyebrows were bushier than Reuben's.

"Yo!" said Reuben, "Robert said you got your knickers in a proper twist."

"Look here you silly twin monkeys, first things first."

I hauled them into the living room.

"Why did you send me those dumb computer messages yesterday?"

I narrowed my eyes and assumed a serious 'don't mess with me' kind of expression. I folded my arms across my chest.

The way the twins stared, made me wonder if I'd spoken Dutch or Swahili.

"The messages?" I repeated, with more emphasis.

"What messages?" asked Robert, bunching his eyebrows together.

"The ones you sent to my computer about needing my help. If that was a joke, it wasn't funny."

"I don't know what you're on about, Michelle," said Robert. "We never sent you any emails yesterday or today. Honest."

Robert looked puzzled. Maybe he was telling the truth. If they didn't send the messages; then maybe it was those aliens after all. Nah! It just couldn't be!

"You guys have lived in this area long enough. Do you know of any computer geeks, hackers or dealers?"

The boys scratched their blond heads.

Robert squinted. "What makes you ask?"

"Wanna hack into your pop's computer?" asked Reuben.

"Well, I—no! Of course not … it's nothing; forget it."

"Look, Michelle, you can't ask something like that and then just clam up. It's not fair," said Robert. His nostrils flared.

"Yeah, either we're your friends, or we're not," chimed in Reuben. "So what will it be?"

This was not the time to make enemies. I took a deep breath and expelled it slowly. "I have to help my dad solve a case, except he doesn't want me involved in it." I paused.

"And?" prompted Robert. "You want to break into his computer?"

"No, not that. I—"

That's when I made up my mind to divulge some of what I knew about the Te Papa robbery, but only after they both took the "no repeating" oath. I omitted the missing security guard, the SIP, and the Sci-fi book, but I began telling them about the weird messages on my computer. We were speaking in low tones when Jason's voice broke in.

"So what're you kids cooking up, now?" He was standing in the kitchen doorway, holding a slice of leftover pizza and a can of coke.

"Who said we're cooking up anything?" I answered.

"Why else would you be whispering?"

"Your computer misses you, Jason," I said.

"Just make sure you don't leave the house unless you tell me. Got that, Mitch P dot I dot? I don't want to have to come searching for you."

Jason stomped off to his room.

"Mitch P dot I dot?" Reuben's eyes were the size of fifty-cent coins. "Who's he?"

"My new name. It's much better than Michelle, PI."

"I'll bet old Bonkers has something to do with this," said Robert, in a serious voice.

"What? Calling Michelle *Mitch*?" asked Reuben.

"No, silly," said Robert. "Dr. Marvel is a scientist, so he would be able to understand a complicated machine."

"I don't believe he's into computers, let alone stealing one," I said

"That doesn't mean anything, Mitch," said Reuben. "We all know how crazy he is, always inventing something or the other. Maybe old Bonkers wants to try his hand at computers, next. Maybe he stole it because he wants to take it apart. If you ask me, I'm sure it was he sending you those messages."

"What exactly were the messages, anyway?" asked Robert.

"Just silly nonsense; nothing worth repeating," I said.

"I say we should go spy on him," said Robert.

"There might be other computer experts living here in Eastbourne," I said. "Why not them?"

"Let's check the Yellow Pages and see how many there are," suggested Reuben.

"Unless they have their own businesses, they won't be listed as computer experts," I pointed out.

I hurried off to fetch the Yellow Pages from the telephone table.

We wrote down the names of three local people who had their own computer businesses: B. L. Shaw of Lowry Bay; F. F. Thompson of Point Howard, and G. Grimm of #35 Moa Road. Suddenly, visions of my collision with G. Grimm on Moa Road flashed through my mind. He and Dr. Marvel had identical house numbers in their addresses, but one lived on Moa Lane, the other on Moa Road!

"So what d'you think, Michelle?" Reuben's squeaky voice jarred me. "Should we go investigate these guys?"

"Shouldn't we be checking out Te Papa? That's where the robbery happened," I said.

The boys shook their heads.

"Reuben and I will check out Dr. Marvel," said Robert, pointing to his brother, "because Jason said that you, Mitch PI, can't leave the house. Remember?"

"That's not what he said. He said I shouldn't leave the house unless I told him. Well, I have a plan and you have to back me up."

I took a deep breath. "Jason!"

"What?" he shouted back.

"I'm going for a bike ride with the twins to Pencarrow Lighthouse, okay?"

"Yeah … okay. No, wait, are Mr. and Mrs. Owen going too?"

"Yep! Come on boys, let's go."

I grabbed my detective notebook and rushed out before Jason could ask any more questions.

Once we reached the garage, Reuben held back, his face long and serious. "Now what?" I said.

"You lied to Jason. It's wrong."

"And I hated doing it, Reuben. But I have to help my father."

I grabbed my bike from the garage, in case Jason decided to check. Once the twins and I reached the bottom of the hill, I dumped it behind the trunk of a Karaka tree.

The twins and I followed the bush route to Dr. Marvel's house. Clutching my notebook, I walked ahead, remembering to dodge the occasional wild rose which reached out with long thorny tentacles to grab unsuspecting victims. Sometimes I forgot to warn the twins, stumbling along behind me, and I could hear them exclaiming "ouch" and "ow" as thorns pricked their exposed body parts or grabbed their sweaters.

Concealed behind shrubs and bushes, we positioned ourselves as close as we could to Dr. Marvel's house. What we were looking for, I wasn't sure. Everything about the house looked normal. No sign of Dr. Marvel anywhere. Maybe he was grocery shopping.

After about twenty minutes, the boys became restless and decided to check out the back of the house.

I remained perched where it was convenient to see the lane and Dr. Marvel's front door. I saw the post-man arrive on his bike and saw him drop some mail in Dr. Marvel's letterbox. Next he rolled his bike across the lane to the house my dad had seemed so interested in last night. A Britz camper-van was parked in the driveway. I was sure it hadn't been there the night before. Did it belong to some out-of-town visitor?

I decided to record that in my notebook.

- *Saturday 24 April. Time—11:15 AM. Place: overlooking Dr. Marvel's. No sign of activity.*

- *11:30 AM—Postman delivered mail.*

- *White Britz camper-van parked in driveway of house opposite—probably visitors.*

A loud fluttering in the branches above my head sent me diving for cover. My heart raced.

When I looked up, I saw a fat woodpigeon fleeing from its perch.

The twins returning must have startled it.

"Hey you guys," I called in a hoarse whisper. "There's nothing more to learn here. Let's move on to plan B."

When neither of them replied, I looked around.

They weren't there! They were probably hiding behind the ferns.

Twelve
Without a Trace

I rushed over to the ferns, parting the branches with my hands.

"Look it, you twin monkeys." I tried not to shout. "This is not the time for messing about."

They weren't there, either.

No giggles, no crunching of dried twigs, nothing.

I searched some more, and after a while, gave up. They must have doubled back and gone home. I was disappointed. Showed you couldn't rely on boys.

I charged back through the bush to where I had dumped my bike, thinking how I would clobber those two when I found them. I had no use for deserters.

I was so preoccupied with my thoughts, I clean forgot about the wild rose brambles, until one tore at my forehead.

"Ouch!"

I would have to add cutters and gloves to my detective bag. The scratch on my forehead stung. I would need to cover it with a band-aid.

I hurried home, expecting to find the twins sitting on our front steps. They weren't. Maybe they were at their house or had gone bike-riding after all. I raced to their front door and rang the bell. Obtaining no answer, I checked their garage. Their bikes were still there. What were those twits up to now?

I hurried home to see if they had phoned.

"Michelle? Back already?" called Jason from his room.

"Forgot my water bottle. Are you still playing games?"

"Nope … composing a new song for the band."

"Jase, did anyone phone while I was gone?"

"Negative, Sherlock. Why? You expecting Dr. Watson?"

"Very funny! Gotta go."

I bolted out the front door, still wondering what could have happened to the twins. Maybe they were with Dr. Marvel and he was showing them his inventions.

I jumped on my bike and raced over to his house again.

The Britz camper was still parked in the driveway opposite.

I dumped my bike on the front lawn and charged up to Dr. Marvel's front door. I jabbed the doorbell. After a long wait, I heard chains rattling; then the door swung open.

"Yes?"

Dr. Marvel's voice was gruff, but when he saw me, his face softened a little. "Oh … ummm … yes …?"

I half expected to see him bound in chains like Marley's ghost.

"Hi, Dr. M, it's Michelle. Have you seen the twins? Are they with you?"

"Twins … what twins? Haven't seen twins, or had double vision this century, Millicent."

Dr. Marvel averted eye contact. His tired, red-rimmed eyes had a dreamy look.

"It's Michelle, Dr. M. Didn't Robert and Reuben stop by to see you?"

"See me? What for? Am I a physician that I should see patients? Go away. I'm busy."

Dr. Marvel folded his arms across his puny chest.

Shifty eyes, and arms folded across the chest—not good, I thought, remembering what I had read earlier in the body language book.

"I'm reading a Sci-fi book called *Sojourners in a World Not Our Own*," I blurted.

That got his attention. He sucked in his breath; his face became flushed.

"What did you say?" He pushed his glasses higher up his nose. "Repeat-a-vous … rewind … repeat!" He cupped his hand to his ear.

"I'm reading a Sci-fi book."

"Yes, yes, yes. What's the title, child?"

"*Sojourners in a World Not Our Own.* Have you …"

"Sojourners … bring me that book, young lady."

"What? Now?"

"Yes, now! Pronto! Hurry … Ummm …"

"Michelle."

"Yes, well yes, yes. Scoot!"

Dr. Marvel half-closed the door; then his head popped out again.

"Don't tell anyone about the book," he whispered. "Now, hurry!" He glanced across the road, before slamming the door shut.

My thoughts went into overdrive as I pedaled home again. Why was Dr. Marvel so anxious to see my book? Why the big mystery? And where were the twins?

Suddenly I remembered Mom's laundry instructions. When I reached home, I raced up the front steps and headed straight for the laundry room.

Jason was there.

"You're back *again?*" said Jason.

"Yeah. I forgot to do Mom's laundry."

"How did you get that scratch?" He stared at my forehead.

"I ploughed into a rose bush. What are you doing?"

"Saving your butt, that's what."

He stuffed a pile of white towels into the washing machine.

"Thanks. I owe you one. Here, I'll take over."

"It's as good as done now. You can hang them on the line, since it's nice and breezy out."

"Yeah, okay."

Jason went to his room.

I could hear him strumming a blues rhythm on his guitar.

I was in big trouble. I had disobeyed Dad, lost the twins, and had been attacked by a deranged rosebush. What else could go wrong?

The shrill blare from the main house telephone made me jump.

The twins!

I raced into the kitchen, grabbed the receiver, before the third ring.

"You silly," I began, intending to give them a good blasting. But something made me halt my onslaught. "Um, hello, Mitch Jones PI speaking."

"Michelle? What are you playing at?"

Oh, no!

Thirteen
Disobedience

"Daaaad?"

"What's with the Mitch PI business?"

"Ummm … huhhh … nothing … just … pretending …"

To admit I was working on his case, after his warning to keep my nose out, would not go down well.

"Listen, honey, I have only a minute to talk. I want you and Jason to catch the bus over to Hutt Cleaners and pick up my Sunday suit."

Dad's timing was bad.

"When? Now? Can't this wait 'til Monday?"

"No, Michelle, today. I need my suit for church tomorrow."

"Can't you wear your blue blazer and gray pants?"

"No!"

"You look so handsome in that blazer, though."

"I expect to find my suit when I get home."

Going to the drycleaners on the bus would take forever. I didn't have forever.

"Can't you pick it up?"

"No!"

"But you'll pass the drycleaners on your way home."

"By the time I'm finished here, they'll be closed."

"Jason is … and I am—"

"Michelle—"

"I'm doing the laundry, and I have to get the things on the line while the sun's out."

"You have enough time to do both."

"But—"

"No more excuses, Fifi. Just do it. Have to go. Oh, one more thing, keep away from Marvel's house."

"Why, Dad?"

"The man is a danger to himself and to society. The lunatic might blow himself up one day and I don't want you there if that happens."

Dad hung up before I could say goodbye. Now I had another dilemma on my hands. Obey Dad or face the consequences.

I must have been staring at the telephone for a full five minutes when I realized that the washing machine had stopped. I decided to do first things first, and that meant hanging the laundry out to dry.

I pulled out the first towel and my jaw dropped. Mom's white towels had blue patches. "Jaaaaason!" I yelled.

No response.

His guitar playing must have a deafening effect, I thought, banging on his bedroom door.

"What, Michelle? Can't you tell I'm practicing?"

"You'd better practice some excuses for when Mom comes home and finds she has blue and white polka-dot towels instead of pure white ones."

The strumming stopped and Jason thundered towards the door. His face was blotchy red. We raced back to the laundry room. Jason rummaged through the wet towels.

"Blast," he said, pulling out his blue rugby shorts from the washer.

"Double blast," I said.

"What can I do, Michelle?"

Apart from the blotches, which had now spread down to his neck, his hands were shaking.

"Got any money?" I said.

"Why?"

"You'd better rush out to Queensgate Mall and buy new towels."

He thumped my shoulder. "Can't we try bleach or something?"

"I don't know if that would work."

We rummaged in the cupboard under the sink until we found a box of detergent meant for stain removal.

We refilled the washer, and put in the recommended measure of the detergent. Jason decided to add some bleach.

"This'd better work," he said under his breath.

I'd never seen my brother so scared. I felt sorry for him.

After half an hour, a still nervous Jason pulled out a towel. It was white again. He turned and hugged me, the wet towel pressed between us.

"You are one lucky so and so, Jason."

If that had been me, I thought, *I would have had to face the firing squad.*

We hung out the towels together.

There was just one more thing to do.

"Jason, Dad wants us to fetch his suit from Hutt Cleaners. I have to see Mrs. Owen about something important. Would you go on your own, please?"

Jason could hardly refuse after I had helped him out of a jam.

I heard the fridge door slam.

"Okay, I'll go when I'm done drinking this."

He sauntered off, slurping down his coke.

The laundry made flapping noises in the wind.

I hurried back indoors, wondering why Teddy hadn't said anything wise to me since he'd encouraged me to break into my father's office and steal confidential information. I went to my room to bug him.

"Listen, O Wise One," I said, but he stared at me with those black unseeing glass eyes. "Say something. You're never this quiet."

Teddy remained silent.

"I always knew you were dumb."

I figured if I taunted him just a little, he would react, but he didn't. I flopped down on the bed. I had lost the twins, and now I had lost communication with my teddy bear. Even though I knew they were really my own thoughts, I still valued the communication.

A tear trickled down my cheek.

"Detectives don't cry."

"Teddy! You're talking again. What happened before?" I wiped my eyes with my sleeve.

"You accused me of causing you to steal confidential information."

I hugged him hard against my chest. "You silly old bear," I whispered close to his stuffed ear. "I need your help. I've lost the twins."

"They're around. You'll find them."

"If you know where they are, tell me."

"Nope. That would be cheating. Besides, if you want to be a good PI you have to find things out on your own."

"If that's how you feel, that's fine."

I replaced Teddy on my pillow, but I wasn't angry. In my heart, I knew I would locate the boys, but I needed to continue my search right away.

"Aren't you forgetting something?" said Teddy.

"What?"

"The book … Dr. Marvel …"

I had forgotten.

I reached down to pick up the Sci-fi book, which was still on my bedroom floor, but drew my hand back, remembering that strange things happened whenever I touched it.

"But, Dr. M wants me to take it to him," I whispered to myself. "All I have to do is grab the book and run like crazy."

I filled my lungs, grabbed the book, and bolted on winged feet.

"Here I go, disobeying Dad yet again!"

"Oi!" said Teddy. "You forgot something else."

"What?"

"Your pops warned you to stay clear of that nut."

"He won't know."

Fourteen
Revelation

"Michelle!"

Half of Jason's body was hanging out his bedroom window.

"Where d'you think you're going now?"

"To see Mrs. Owen. I told you."

I scampered into the garage, got my bike, and charged down the hill like a wild boar. By the time I reached Dr. Marvel's driveway, I was breathless. The Britz camper-van was still parked in the driveway across the road.

I dumped my bike on the lawn and charged up Dr, Marvel's front steps. All the drapes at the front of the house were drawn, though I was sure they had been open when I called on him earlier. I pressed the doorbell, but there was no response. I was about to press the bell again when I heard a hoarse whisper from the other side of the door.

"Go to the back door, Marilyn."

"It's Michelle, Dr. Marvel," I said, leaning close to the door. "Michelle."

"Whatever. Got the book?"

"Yes."

"Good. Now, go to the back door—hurry!"

What was wrong with letting me in the front door?

Half annoyed, I scampered down the steps and followed the concrete path, leading round to the back. Dr. Marvel was already there holding the door open, just wide enough for me to squeeze through. His dingy, white lab-coat hung lopsidedly over his baggy corduroy pants and striped flannel shirt. His socked feet were encased in plastic shopping bags. His hair was ruffled and in need of combing.

The smell of sardines made me sneeze.

"Goshwalladite," said Dr. Marvel, grabbing a can of air freshener and emptying it as he squelched around in his plastic-bag shoes trying to kill the odor.

He flung the empty container into the rubbish bin under the kitchen sink, before ushering me into the darkened living room.

I sneezed a few more times.

"Goshwalladite, m'lady," he said again.

"Goshwalla … what?" I asked.

"It means bless you," said Dr. Marvel. "Russian, Greek, Swahili, or something."

"You mean Gesund-heit?"

"Whatever."

"It's German."

Dr. Marvel spun around as if expecting someone to spring at him.

"German … here … what—?" he said in a hoarse whisper.

When he saw my startled look, he pulled his shoulders back and smiled.

"Just joking, Little Bo Peep, just joking."

It wasn't surprising that Dr. Marvel was jumpy. His living room was in a shambles. A variety of clothes, books, newspapers, dishes, cushions, telescopes, compasses, and other miscellaneous paraphernalia lay scattered over the floor and on every flat surface. A plumb line dangled from the end of the TV aerial. This was most peculiar.

"What's going on, Dr. M? What's all this? Aren't you going to open your drapes to let in sunlight? What about cracking open a window to let in some fresh air?"

"Eh? Break my window? Do you know what replacement glass costs?"

"I said … never mind, Dr. M."

I stepped over several books, but could not avoid landing on a plate containing what was left of Dr. Marvel's sardine and potato lunch.

"Is this why you're wearing plastic bags over your socks?"

Dr. Marvel's jaw dropped, and he gawked at me as if I were the demented one.

"What?"

He placed his bony fists on his hipbones and assumed a round-back stance. He reminded me of a giant kidney bean.

"You dare question my footwear, Millicent?"

I removed my foot from the plate, shaking off some mashed potato.

Dr. Marvel stared at me wide-eyed.

Knots formed in my tummy.

"Should … should I come back at another … er … more convenient time, Dr. M?"

My palms were sweaty and the book slipped out of my hand, landing on the bare wooden floor with a thud.

"Bombs! Take cover!" yelled Dr. Marvel, diving under the dining table, hands pressed against his ears, his backside sticking up in the air.

I tried not to laugh.

"I dropped the book, Dr. M, the book you wanted to see."

In a flash Dr. Marvel straightened up. The top of his head narrowly missed contact with the edge of the table.

"I knew that."

He adjusted his lab-coat.

"I was just testing your ability to react in a crisis situation. One must always be prepared, you know … in case the sirens go off. Ah, yes, the book."

Trembling hands reached for it.

I'd never seen Dr. Marvel look so scared. From the way he stared at the front cover, I thought he would be sucked right into the picture. He plopped himself onto the sofa, combed his fingers through his hair.

"Sit, Marietta—" His voice trembled a little.

I sat on the edge of the sofa.

"Michelle. My name is Michelle."

"Yes, yes, whatever. Will you stop interrupting?"

"Sorry!"

I adjusted my breathing to match the slow swing of the pendulum on the cuckoo clock; tick—tock—tick—tock—tick.

"Are you going to read it, or what?" I blurted.

I clammed up when Dr. Marvel pinned me with a one-eyed stare. I pretended to count all the weird apparatus around the room, bobbing my head as I went.

"And stop that infernal nodding, will you? Can't you sit still?" said Dr. Marvel, before lapsing into silence again.

"Sorry!" I folded my arms across my chest.

Out of the corner of my eye, I saw Dr. Marvel comb his fingers through his messy hair, again. When he cleared his throat with a grating sound, I jumped.

"I had an unusual visitation last night, Mildred …" he began in a dignified voice, sounding like those posh English people who speak as if they have a mouthful of marbles—except he was from Texas.

"It was the hour when I usually seek rest and repose, the hour when I succumb to the power of Wynken, Blynken, and … Moo …"

"Nod—oops, sorry." I clapped my hand over my mouth.

"Whatever. As I was saying, I laid prostrate upon my four-poster, king-sized support unit, with the thick goose-down whats-it atop me. I still couldn't succumb to those three rascals, Wynken, Blynken, and … and …"

I mouthed "Nod" when he shot me a help-me-out glance.

"Nod," he cleared his throat. "So I performed the only guaranteed method of encouraging those rascals. I got up and shuffled over to my recliner, thereupon I deposited my posterior, and reached for my novel.

"Alas, *Beyond The Twenty-third Century*—the book I had been reading—was not the book I picked up, not the book I had been reading the night before, that is. Of this, I was certain. But the book I held, *Sojourners in a World Not Our Own*—this very book which I now hold—was the one I had picked up."

Dr. Marvel held up my book, waving it about like an animated preacher in a pulpit. I was making an effort not to laugh, for I had never seen him express himself in such a frantic manner. It took me a minute or two to sort out what he was trying to tell me.

With his free hand, Dr. Marvel reached into the deep pocket of his labcoat and extracted a book. It was identical to mine. I gasped but said nothing, realizing that the village library might well have a few copies available.

Taking a deep breath, a much calmer Dr. Marvel continued: "Who in the name of Neptune's gray beard had betook my book? I stared at the spot where I had last seen it. Who could have done this dastardly thing? Who indeed! For I, as you know, Millie-girl, live alone. Thereupon, I contemplated the cover of this here book, and I felt compelled to peruse the first chapter. I was transfixed—no, spellbound more like—as the story unfolded. Listen to this, Madeline."

Dr. Marvel opened his copy of *Sojourners in a World Not Our Own* and proceeded to read the first chapter aloud. I would have stopped him because I had already read the same chapter, but I knew he wouldn't appreciate the interruption. When he read the part that said "There are two on Earth who can help us, one is old, he must find the other" I sat bolt upright, my nerves tingling. I was certain the words in my book were "… one is *young, she* must find the other."

"What transpired next still baffles me …" continued Dr. Marvel, closing the book. He pursed his lips and rubbed the side of his jaw with his shoulder. Then he became silent!

It took sheer willpower to resist the urge to prod him back into talking mode. If he stayed silent for ten inhalations, I would have no choice but to poke him in the ribs.

By the time I counted to eight, Dr. Marvel stirred.

"What transpired next still confounds me," he said. "It was like … a vision … hmmm, no … more like a visitation … yes, a visitation! Two apparitions shimmered before me, vague they were, not quite clear. They struggled, trying to maintain their vapory presence. So in a stern voice I commanded 'Stand still and deliver. Have you come in response to my space-beam signals? Or are you the ghosts of Marley and Scrooge?'

"They wavered about some more, like flags in a gentle wind. Then, as if drawing upon the last of their energy, one came more clearly into focus. To my surprise, one spoke. 'Need help … find other … too weak … Boraz.'

"Then, pop, just like that, they disappeared, gone, vanished. Well, that jolted me out of my stupor, I can tell you. I must have been dreaming with my eyes open, I told myself."

Dr. Marvel finished at last.

The name Boraz made my head tingle. I began to remember my dream. I was anxious to share this with Dr. Marvel, but didn't want to risk interrupting his moment of reflection.

When he looked at me and nodded, I knew it was my turn to speak.

"Dr. M, I had a similar experience. Well, what I mean is, Boraz and his companion, Arkon, are from another planet. In my book it says, one is *young*, *she* must find the other."

At this, Dr. Marvel sucked in his breath and narrowed his eyes, making his bushy eyebrows peak at the center of his forehead.

"Expound, Melanie, expound! Waste not another nanosecond!" he said.

"Here, let me show you." I took my copy of the book and flicked to the page. "There, see."

Dr. Marvel peered at the words; then said, "Tell me your dream, child."

I told him about my dream and about the weird messages on my computer screen but I omitted everything concerning the SIP and Mr. Ihaka. I didn't want to complicate things.

"… and now this, Dr. M! What are we supposed to do?"

"Do, Margaret? It's obvious you and I are the ones they speak of in these books. They desire help. Humbug! So it wasn't my intricate experiment that brought them."

"What intricate experiment is that?"

I looked at the plumb line tied to his TV aerial, and the long, thin wire connected to the end of the aerial, which ran along the wooden floor, and disappeared up the chimney.

Nothing state-of-the-art, that's for sure!

"Did I say experiment? Huuum, what I mean is—fiddlesticks, I don't know what I mean, Millicent."

Dr. Marvel waved both arms in the air. The two books he was holding slammed together. Lights sprayed out like sparkles from a firecracker. He sat as if glued to the sofa, unable to pull the books apart. His white hair glowed different colors from the reflected light of the sparkles; his eyes bulged, his glasses slipped off his nose and dangled from one ear.

The lights gathered as if being sucked by a powerful vacuum cleaner; then swooped under the sofa. The fireworks stopped; the books fell out of Dr. Marvel's hands and vanished before reaching the floor.

"At last …" said a thin voice, barely audible. "We were beginning to wonder how much longer we had to wait for you two to find each other."

Fifteen
Boraz

"What did you say, Marge?" said Dr. Marvel.

"I … noth … nothing—"

"You could bowl me over with a handful of cotton balls." Dr. Marvel was shaking like a leaf. "Do you know what just happened here, Millie-girl?"

"Contact, that's what," said a voice, from somewhere around Dr. Marvel's feet.

The voice startled us again.

I sprang up and did a hop on one foot.

Dr. Marvel pressed his back into the sofa and hoisted his feet high into the air. His eyes bulged and his face turned beet red.

From beneath the sofa, a hazy blue light flickered. It extended upwards, before it shimmered into a humanoid shape.

Dr. Marvel and I gasped at the same time.

"Who … what … are you?" said Dr. Marvel, a quiver in his voice. His raised feet crashed to the ground and he sprang up like jack-in-the-box. His legs wobbled so much he had to brace them against the front edge of the sofa.

"We owe much to you, curious scientist. The laser beam you projected into outer space guided our hasty escape to Earth."

Dr. Marvel stared at his weird equipment, his eyes following the connection of wires to the brick fireplace, before he returned his gaze to the apparition.

"It worked? My cockamamie experiment worked? Are you a Martian?"

"Negative! Zorbian. My name is Boraz."

"Boraz?" Both Dr. Marvel and I echoed.

"Yes. We meet again, dear Michelle," said Boraz.

I blushed.

"I haven't much time to explain things here," continued Boraz, becoming more visible. "Not enough energy to sustain this state. Come to Te Papa at about this time, tomorrow. Arkon and I will talk with you there."

I checked my watch; it was just after two.

"But how do we find you?" I asked, recovering my voice.

Although Boraz's face looked humanoid, there was something missing. Eyebrows and eyelashes! He had none. Even so, he looked quite human. That's when I noticed he wore no clothes either.

I gasped.

Dr. Marvel must have noticed too, because he grabbed two cushions.

"For goodness sake, man … or whatever you are … wear this."

Dr. Marvel planted one cushion in front of Boraz's dangling private bits; the other he stuck in my face.

"You can't go around exposing yourself to all and sundry."

"Exposing … all and sundry?" said Boraz.

"Naked, man, naked!" said Dr. Marvel, his voice almost shrill. "There's a girl child here, see. Hold that object where I placed it, Mr. Boraz."

Still holding the other cushion to my face, Dr. Marvel rotated me with his free hand so that I faced the back wall of the living room. I offered no resistance; I was too embarrassed.

"Now, Mr. Boraz," said Dr. Marvel, "you'd better put this on."

"Ah! Yes, I see," said Boraz. "Do I have need of your unusual foot attire, too?"

"Negative, Mr. Boraz," said Dr. Marvel.

"And it's just Boraz … you can drop the Mister."

"As you wish," said Dr. Marvel. "Now, child, it's safe for you to turn around."

Boraz was clad in Dr. Marvel's lab-coat, which reached to just above his kneecaps for he was much taller. His legs were hairy and spindly but they terminated in platypus-like feet.

Yikes!

"Will you look like that when we see you at Te Papa?" I asked, staring at his unusual feet.

"No. But don't worry. Arkon and I will find you." Boraz flickered. "It's critical that we meet to talk about the S1M1 unit. It's a matter of life and death. It …"

"It … what?" urged Dr. Marvel, as Boraz's voice trailed off.

"It has been …" said Boraz faintly.

With a pop, the blue light extinguished. Boraz was gone. The borrowed lab-coat he was wearing crumpled to the floor.

Dr. Marvel and I stared at each other. He burst out laughing.

"Darn! Mr. Boraz … Boraz without the Mister. What's in a name, Millie-girl?"

Dr. Marvel, his arms flapping about like a bird, sprang off the sofa. He began a series of pirouettes around the room, which made me think, with all the excitement, he had finally lost the rest of his marbles.

"What was he about to tell us about the S1M1 unit, child? It has been … something … what something … something what?"

Wobbling from his energetic acrobatics, Dr. Marvel looked at me with giddy eyes.

"Young Michelle, we have much work to do. We have to find out what this Boraz wants from us. I'll bet he's from Mars or Jupiter or … flaming orbiting asteroids, what does it matter where he's from! Fact remains … he was here … is here … somewhere."

It was difficult to erase the image of Boraz's dangling parts from my mind.

"He's from planet Zorb, remember?" I said. "Their planet has not yet been discovered by man."

"Whatever. We—rather I, have made contact with aliens, and we—as in me and you—have to find out what they want to tell us about their S1M1 unit."

"It might be dangerous to do that, Dr. M. We don't really know anything about these beings or the power of their unit. They might be villains. They might even be looking for strange humans to dissect. Besides, I have an even more serious problem on my hands. The twins, Reuben and Robert, have disappeared … vanished into thin air, abducted even."

This brought Dr. Marvel to a standstill, or as close to reality as he was likely to get. He tilted his head.

"Millie-girl, people don't just disappear into thin air. It ain't possible."

He flopped onto the sofa as if exhausted.

"Boraz did."

"That's different. He's from outer space. For him that sort of thing is second nature."

Dr. Marvel drew in a deep breath, filling his tummy like a balloon and his cheeks like a puffed-up toad. The air whistled when he expelled it through fluttering lips.

"Where were those boys when you last saw them?" he asked, running his bony fingers through his bushy hair.

Spying on you! I almost blurted.

A frantic banging at the front door startled us.

Sixteen
The Twins Turn Up

"Now what?" said Dr. Marvel, springing off the sofa like a kangaroo.

He stepped, as if on eggshells, towards the front door. He grabbed an empty drinking glass from a nearby table and placed the bottom to his ear. Beckoning me to be quiet, he pressed the open end of the glass against the inside of the door. Whatever he heard caused an instant reaction. He yanked the door open and hauled two stunned boys inside.

"If it isn't Fred and Barney!" Dr. Marvel slammed the door shut.

"Reuben! Robert!" I blurted, scrambling off the sofa.

"Two book-ends for the price of one," said Dr. Marvel, staring at the boys.

I was more relieved than angry. "What are you doing here? I mean, where have you been? I thought you'd disappeared."

The twins looked scared out of their wits. Reuben wasn't wearing his red sweater anymore, only his black roll-neck jersey.

"I … we … um," began Reuben, struggling to breathe. "You tell, Robert. I'm still spooked."

"Yes, do tell," encouraged Dr. Marvel, guiding the boys by their shoulders and sitting them on the sofa. "Nice and slow. That's it … breathe easy. Now, what has happened to put you in this turbulent state?"

Taking a deep breath, Robert glanced at the draped windows; then around the room before he spoke.

"We were chased by an angry man."

"Eh?" said Dr. Marvel, his eyes narrowed.

"He's kidding, Dr. M. These twin monkeys like to—"

"We're not, Michelle. We were chased," said Robert in a stern voice.

"Sorry …"

"The man thought we were fish," said Reuben.

"Eh?" repeated Dr. Marvel. "Make sense, boy. Fish don't swim on land."

The twins were still winded. Maybe they were telling the truth.

"Who chased you, then?" I asked.

"Dunno. Me and Reuben were crouching close to the window when the kitchen door flew open and a man came storming out. His intentions were obvious, I can tell you."

"Back up a bit, Robert," I said. "None of this makes sense. Where were you? Whose window are you talking about?"

"Well, while you were spying on … er … old Bonkers, Reuben and I decided to check on Professor Grimm—"

"Grimm?" Dr. Marvel butted in. "Why him? Why spy on him? And who is this Bonkers? Bonkers … doesn't ring a bell. Should I know him? Never heard of him. Where does he live? What does he do? With a name like that, he's probably bonkers no doubt."

The twins and I exchanged sly glances, trying not to laugh.

"Do you know anything about Professor Grimm?" I asked Dr. Marvel.

"Not much, except he's an accomplished computer designer or engineer—but everyone is an engineer these days, even rubbish collectors." Dr. Marvel cleared his throat. "Grimm lives at 35 Moa Road, I believe."

"I think I knocked him over with my bike yesterday, just outside his house," I said.

"Think? Either you knocked him over or you didn't. Which was it?" said Dr. Marvel.

"The man I knocked over went into 35 Moa Road. I assumed it must be Grimm, but I have to admit, I'd never seen him before. All the same, the man was furious."

Dr. Marvel laughed. "Who wouldn't be after being ploughed into by a wild cyclist? Bet he had the stuffing knocked clean out of him."

"He might have been angry with me, but he was sure acting suspicious."

"Suspicious?" Dr. Marvel remained thoughtful. "Why do you say that, Marilyn?"

I shrugged. "Dunno, just a feeling."

We lapsed into silence, but not for long.

I was still anxious to know all that had happened to the twins.

"So, Robert, was it Grimm who chased you?"

Robert took a deep breath. "Nope, but you know how the hill slopes down the other side of the lane—close to the back of Professor Grimm's house?

Well, Reuben and I were half-way down the slope when we saw a man wearing a wide-brimmed straw hat hobbling along the path to Professor Grimm's
back steps. We ducked behind a Ngaio tree just as the man reached the door.
He banged on it a couple of times before it opened."

"'Any progress, Grimm?' the man demanded," chimed in Reuben.

"Professor Grimm answered, 'Not much. Did you bring what I asked for?'"
said Robert.

"And when the man went inside, we snuck up close to the window again,"
said Reuben.

"We couldn't hear clearly what they were saying. Their voices were muffled," said Robert. "Reuben spotted one of those small trapdoors that let pets
into the house. Just as he was poking the flap open with his head, the kitchen
door flew open again and the strange man charged out. Boy, he looked mad.
The man sniffed the air and told Grimm he could smell fish. His eyes darted
like a firefly. Then he said, 'When I smell fish, something's fishy.'"

"That's when Professor Grimm came outside and said 'If it smells fishy out
here, then someone's cooking fish. Goodbye and have a nice day.' Then he
went back inside and banged the door shut, leaving the other man still sniffing
the air."

"And then what happened?" I asked.

Robert swallowed. "'Run!' I yelled to Reuben, kicking him in the backside.
I bolted. When I looked back, Reuben's head was still stuck in the trapdoor
opening. The man was charging down the steps. There was only way to stall
him. I picked up a rock and tossed it at his kneecaps. He dodged the rock, but
missed the bottom step and tumbled to the ground. This allowed me to tug
Reuben free. We dashed towards the Ngaio tree."

"Then what happened?" I prompted.

"I thought for sure the man had hurt himself when he tumbled down the
steps, but the next thing I knew, he was yelling and charging after us. We
didn't hang around, we raced for the hill, but Reuben tripped." Robert broke
into giggles.

"You wouldn't be grinning if it were you," said Reuben elbowing his
brother.

"I heard Reuben yelp. I looked back. The man had grabbed hold of his
sweater. Without thinking, I scrambled down the slope and kicked the man's
shin just as Reuben slipped out of his sweater. The man said a nasty word and
hobbled after us. Reuben and I pelted up the side of the hill like Spiderman,

leaving the angry man rubbing his shin with one hand, while swinging Reuben's sweater in the air with the other."

"But you two were gone for ages?" I said.

"We were watching the house, before all this happened. That's what detectives do—stalk suspicious characters, until something happens," said Reuben.

"Detectives? You!" I said with sarcasm.

"Why not?" challenged Robert.

"Stalking Grimm! But why?" piped up Dr. Marvel. "The little I know of the man, he wouldn't hurt a fly's behind. What is he supposed to have done that warranted spying?"

"It's just a game they were playing, Dr. M," I jumped in, before the twins could tell him about our list of possible suspects, of which he was one.

"Anyway," Robert continued, "Reuben and I lost that lunatic in the bush. He was too fat to come after us."

Robert smiled and leaned back on the sofa.

"Do you remember what the man looked like?" I asked.

"Not too much, except he was short-ish, fat-ish, and walked funny, like his shoes were too tight. We couldn't see his face because of his hat." Reuben clasped his hands.

My mind spun like a spinning wheel gone mad. From Reuben's description, the man could well have been Mr. Ihaka, except that wouldn't make sense. But what if there was a connection between the SIP, Boraz, and Mr. Ihaka? Was it possible Professor Grimm was involved, too? But Dr. Marvel had said he wouldn't hurt a fly's bottom.

This was getting complicated. There were too many unanswered questions. How I wished I could talk to Dad.

"Wake up, wake up. I'm talking to you, M'lady." Dr. Marvel was standing in front of me waving his hand in my face. "Do these boys know anything about you-know-who-from-you-know-where?"

"Uh? What?"

"Do these boys know—"

"Yeah, I heard you, Dr. M." I had to shut him up fast before he spilled too much. "Yes, they know—wait, not everything."

"Meaning?" said Dr. Marvel.

I pulled him to one side and whispered in his ear. "Nothing about you-know-who, because at the time I didn't remember my vis … dream." My jaws ached from clenching them so tight.

"Then they must be told," said Dr. Marvel.

"No. It would only make them more curious. We don't really want them involved, do we?"

Dr. Marvel pondered that for a moment; then he rushed over to his large Rimu-wood desk, shuffled some papers, and came back with two black wrist straps. He rubbed them against his coat sleeves.

"These are secrecy bands," he said aloud.

"Secrecy bands?" said Robert, craning his neck.

"Yes. My latest invention, though I haven't exactly tested them yet. I've wanted to do so for some time."

"How could plastic straps make anyone keep a secret?" asked Reuben, with a grin.

"My boy," said Dr. Marvel, squaring his shoulders. "Anyone wearing these gizmos will never be able to divulge a single secret, unless the bands are removed—surgically."

"So what's to stop a pair of scissors?" I asked.

"Ah," said Dr. Marvel, stabbing the air with his right index finger. "That's where my genius comes in. I have designed these bands to be impenetrable. It is only I who can remove them, and that is my secret, Millie-girl."

To me, the bands looked like ordinary plastic watchbands with buckles and holes.

"You don't need a rocket scientist to undo a simple strap like that, do you, Dr. M?" I asked.

"Let's see what the boys think, shall we?" He rushed over to them. "Now boys, the young detective and I will divulge what we know of this extraordinary affair, but only if you agree to wear these bands."

The twins' eyes lit up.

"We agree to everything you said, Dr. Marvel," said Robert. "We promise not to blab or meddle anymore."

"That'd be a first for you. Nothing ever keeps you quiet," said Reuben.

"Shush." Robert jabbed his brother with his elbow. "We will wear your invention, Dr. Marvel, after you tell us the juicy bits."

"There you are, Miss Millicent. They agree. Now we can tell them. A problem shared is a problem halved. In this case it's a problem quartered. Get it?"

"But Dr. M, the books never said anything about four ... only two," I said.

"Look it here, Michelle," said Robert, "stop stalling. We said we'd wear the secrecy bands."

"Yeah, spit it out," said Reuben. "Who's this 'you-know-who-from-you-know-where'?"

Against my better judgment, Dr. Marvel and I took turns telling the twins about our alien visitors, and that we were going to meet them at Te Papa to learn more about their S1M1 unit.

The boys sat on the edge of their chairs, their eyeballs growing larger and larger.

"Wow!" said Reuben. "You mean real aliens are here in New Zealand, but only you two get to see them?"

Robert, though, had a skeptical frown on his face.

"Yeah, right. What did you have for breakfast, Michelle? Space balls?"

"It's no use talking to skeptics," I said. "I'm surprised at you, Robert, especially after what I told you two before. Well, whether you believe it or not, Boraz and Arkon are real aliens from planet Zorb, and they want me and Dr. M to help them."

"No need to puff up like a blowfish, Michelle," said Robert, pulling his shoulders back. "If it's true what you two said, then this means you have two cases to solve."

"So?"

"Well, while you and Dr. Marvel meet with these *so-called* aliens at Te Papa to learn about their S1-whatever unit, Reuben and I could continue to spy on Professor Grimm. Don't you see? We can be useful."

"Sorry boys," said Dr. Marvel. "Too many cabbages make stinky soup. After your narrow escape, it's best that you don't remember any of this."

Dr. Marvel attached the bands on the twins' right wrists. Then he looked them in the eyes.

"And you will keep your sniffers tuned to things other than snooping ... so this case, or spying on Grimm, no longer concerns you," he said.

He grinned at me and rubbed his hands together.

"A little hypnotic suggestion can't hurt, can it, young Mitch?"

"Yeah, but you said it after the bands were on. Will it still work?" I asked.

"Will it still work, Millie-girl? Of course! Observe. Boys, remove the bands."

The twins yanked at the bands but couldn't undo them. The free ends of the bands had self-sealed, forming a continuous circle around their wrists.

Dr. Marvel coughed. "No point trying to hacksaw them, either. You might end up with no wrists."

There was a sparkle in his eyes and a satisfied grin spread across his lips. I wondered whether he was telling everything about the strap.

"Now for the memory test." Dr. Marvel cleared his throat. "Boys, what does the word S1M1 mean to you?"

Reuben rolled his eyes. "That's not a word, Dr. M, just two letters followed by number 1."

"Are you developing a new mathematical equation?" asked Robert. "Is S1M1 the same as SM squared?"

"Excellent! Excellent!" said Dr. Marvel, clapping his hands. "What does Zorb mean to you?"

The twins laughed.

"Zorb is a large inflated plastic sphere with another sphere inside. You strap yourself in and then roll down the hill like a twit," said Robert.

"It's a crazy Kiwi sporting invention for dumb tourists," said Reuben.

Dr. Marvel slapped the side of his leg. "Yeees! And tell me … tell me, what do you know about Boraz?"

"What's that?" said Reuben. "Another invention?"

"Do you mean borsch, Dr. Marvel? That's a Russian soup based on beetroot," said Robert, the smarter of the twins. "No, wait a minute, that can't be it. You have a dog, a dog with a long silky coat. That's it, isn't it? You have a Boraz." Robert jumped up. "Show us the dog, please Dr. Marvel. My brother and I love dogs."

Dr. Marvel threw his head back and laughed. "That's a borzoi, boy, b-o-r-z-o-i. I said Boraz—B-o-r-a-z. Oh, never mind."

There was sheer satisfaction on Dr. Marvel's face.

"You forgot about the hypnotic thing, Dr. M," I whispered.

"Ah, yes. Tell me, boys, will you continue snooping?"

The twins exchanged glances, before moving their heads in slow motion, their eyes staring past Dr. Marvel.

"We … know … of … nothing … that … requires … snooping."

They spoke in unison, as if they were robots.

I was skeptical about their sincerity. I waved my hand in front of their faces, but they seemed to be in a daze.

While the twins stared into space, Dr. Marvel and I made plans to visit Te Papa. I would tell my parents that he was helping me with my science project and that we needed to go to the museum to look at the model of the solar system on display there.

"Great, Dr. M," I said. "See you tomorrow."

"Good. Now I must release the twins."

When Dr. Marvel snapped his fingers, the boys jerked back to normal.

"You guys okay?" I asked.

Robert scratched his head. "Yeah, Michelle, you two were gonna to tell us something about—what were they gonna tell us, Reuben?"

"Dunno," said Reuben. "Were you going to tell us something?" He looked at me then Dr. Marvel.

"Nope!" I said quickly, jumping to my feet. "But it's time we left. Bye Dr. M."

I bolted for the door, the twins stumbling behind.

"Hey!" Dr. Marvel called after us. "What about this Bonkers chap?"

We pretended not to hear.

Just then, it started to drizzle.

"Oh, no," I said, "Mom's laundry!"

The rain was pelting down by the time we reached the end of Dr. Marvel's driveway. The wind, too, was picking up speed. Dry leaves and twigs swirled everywhere like creepy-crawly spiders. The twins scampered ahead of me.

The Britz camper-van was still parked in the driveway opposite. I wondered if it had moved at all since I saw it yesterday. It seemed like a waste of money to rent a motorized camper, only to have it sit in the driveway. I squinted to see if anyone might be inside, but the windows were too dark.

I picked up my soaking wet bike. Straddling it, I pushed off for home, shooting past the twins, who were jogging along, huddling against the merciless wind and giggling with each other.

"We're glad we don't know nothing, Mitch, PI," I heard them shout.

"Have you seen Dr. Marvel's new dog called Boraz?" shouted Robert.

Boy, I sure hope the secrecy bands worked!

Seventeen
Outsmarting Dad

A loud, persistent banging on my bedroom door woke me the following morning.

"Wake up, P dot I dot. You don't want to be late for church, do you?" shouted Jason.

"Stop banging, Neanderthal. Go away."

Instead, he came in.

"Michelle, listen up. I've got bad news."

Jason flopped on the end of my bed.

"What bad news? Oh I know … your friends got arrested for making the racket you call music. Now the cops are after you, too. You're going into hiding and you want me to cover for you. That's it, right?"

"I wish it was that simple," said Jason, hanging his head.

"What's up?" I pushed the covers back and knelt beside him. "Did you break a string on your guitar? Or did your imaginary girlfriend dump you?"

"I forgot to pick up Dad's suit yesterday."

"You didn't!"

Jason's head jerked up and down. "Yep!"

"Thanks a lot." I slumped cross-legged beside him. "Dad's going to be pretty ticked off. So what do we tell him?"

"We? Nah-ah, Michelle. You. What are *you* going to tell him."

"You can't do this, Jason. You can't leave me to face him on my own."

"What good will it do if we both get grounded, eh?"

"After I saved your butt from ruining Mom's towels yesterday, you let me down like this. That's not nice."

I fired a punch at his arm, but he sprang out of reach. At the door, he turned, and with a shrug said, "Sorry, Mitch P dot I dot."

"PI, Jason, not P dot I, okay?"

I dragged myself out of bed and made a beeline for the bathroom. The clock struck eight, just as I finished dressing for church. I had ten minutes to wolf down my breakfast.

Dad, wearing his blue blazer and gray pants, was still at the breakfast table. He kept looking at me with one eyebrow raised, his lips pursed.

"Is it about your suit, Dad?" I said, eyeing him over the top of my half-raised spoon. "Sorry."

"Well—"

"It rained too much, Dad. It's no fun getting all wet walking to the bus and stuff. And Mom's laundry got all soaked."

"And why was that, Michelle? Didn't you have enough time to bring it in before the downpour?"

Dad was angry.

"It's not my fault that the weather here is so unpredictable, Dad."

"Where were you?"

I knew I had to come clean.

"At Dr. Marvel's …"

"Why? Didn't I specifically tell you to stay away from that lunatic?"

Here was my chance.

"I asked him to help me with my science project. You know, the one on planets …" I shoveled a spoonful of cereal into my mouth.

"Pardon?" Dad raised one eyebrow, and folded his arms across his chest.

I chewed on my top lip. He wouldn't like this next bit.

"Dr. M thinks we should go over to Te Papa to look at an actual display of the planets, something about a tenth planet."

"A tenth what?"

"Planet. Dr. M thinks there's one hovering around our solar system. This could really, really help my project—and earn me a B plus. We might even become famous. Can I go, Dad? Can I? Please?"

I swallowed the last bit of my cereal and washed it down with a mouthful of Dad's lukewarm coffee.

"No! Marvel is stuffing your head with a load of nonsense, Michelle." Dad wasn't smiling.

I could almost hear wheels grinding in his head as he tried to comprehend what I had said. *Michelle, Dr. Marvel, a tenth planet, Te Papa … doesn't add up!*

I was sure he suspected I had been snooping around for answers on the "forbidden" case.

Dad's dead clever where I am concerned. He knows how my mind works.

Anytime now, smoke would spew from his ears like an angry volcano. I had to be careful with my resolve to outsmart him.

Dad leaned his elbows on the table, his eyes boring into mine.

"What exactly are you up to, Michelle? Why would Marvel take the trouble to accompany you to Te Papa to show you a planet which doesn't exist?"

"Eh? Well, I—"

Fight the temptation to tell the truth, Michelle.

A lingering cornflake at the back of my throat made me cough. I reached for Dad's coffee again and drained it.

"I'm waiting."

"I just told you, Dad, he's helping me with my project. If he thinks there's a tenth planet out there, who am I to dispute it? Besides, Te Papa has an incredible multimedia database." I crossed my fingers under the table.

"What makes me curious, Michelle, is why he would take you to the museum rather than the observatory to research this so-called tenth planet."

Good question! One I hadn't considered.

Dad leaned forward, waiting for me to squeeze my way out of this one.

Mom poked her head through the doorway to the dining room.

"Honey, if Dr. Marvel wants to take her to Te Papa, I see nothing wrong with that. He's a scientist, and she has a science project. No more needs to be said, does it?"

Thanks Mom!

Dad leaned back in his chair, and shoved his thumbs into his waistband.

"But the man is a lunatic. Everyone knows that. I can't believe you could be so casual about Michelle hanging around him, let alone spending time with him at the museum exploring a non-existent planet."

His mellow voice was edged with controlled anger.

Mom laughed. "Dr. Marvel's no lunatic, honey, eccentric, yes, but no lunatic."

Dad scratched the back of his head. "Fine, but this tenth planet I gotta see."

Me too, I thought, as I gathered the empty breakfast dishes and scampered off to the kitchen.

Just before we left for church, I phoned Dr. Marvel and told him the good news. We agreed to catch the one o'clock ferry.

"You'd better chalk up an 'A' for that project," Dad whispered in my ear, just as I hung up.

By the time we returned from church and had lunch, Dad had calmed down. With only fifteen minutes to catch the ferry, he surprised me by offering to give me a ride down to the dock. He had a carry-on bag slung over his shoulder.

"What's in the bag, Dad?"

"Stuff ... just stuff. Let's go."

Mom waved from the window.

Dad nosed down the road to Dr. Marvel's house and tooted the horn. The front door swung open. Dr. Marvel skipped down the steps and along his driveway towards us. He looked smart in a blue pinstripe suit. For once, his hair was neatly combed—flattened with tons of jell. He was clean-shaven except for his bushy moustache. He carried a tattered brown leather briefcase under one arm. In contrast, I was wearing a washed-out pair of blue jeans, an oversized navy sweater, and my *special* detective running shoes.

"Your date," teased Dad, as Dr. Marvel hurried towards us. "And dressed for the occasion, so he is." Dad chuckled.

I poked him in the ribs. "Dad, don't be sarcastic," I said through clenched teeth.

I smiled and waved to Dr. Marvel.

He climbed into the rear seat, bringing with him a strong aroma of Old Spice and mothballs.

"A lovely day for a sail across the harbor," he said, cradling his briefcase.

"You look very ... er ... handsome, Dr. M," I said.

Dad cleared his throat.

"I must look the part, little one," said Dr. Marvel, flicking fluff off his sleeve.

"The part?" said Dad, one eyebrow raised.

"Yes," said Dr. Marvel. "We scientists must always look as if we're all about business, if you know what I mean, Mr.... er ..."

"Jones, detective Jones, senior," I helped.

"Detective Jones, of course ..."

Dad pulled into a parking space close to the boatshed at Days Bay.

"Here we are," he said.

Dr. Marvel and I climbed out.

"How much do I owe you, young man?" said Dr. Marvel, fumbling in his pocket.

He pulled out a faded black leather wallet.

"It's complimentary," said Dad, rolling his eyes upwards.

"In that case … aloha!"

Dr. Marvel stuffed the wallet back into his jacket pocket.

We waved to Dad and hurried down the length of the wharf to the waiting ferry.

The ferry departed on time.

Through the salt-streaked glass windows, I could see Dad's Land Rover speeding away, as if he was in a big hurry to get some place. Except for Dr. Marvel and me, there were only two other passengers on the ferry. Both men had deep suntans and a full growth of beard. They were busy poring over a map or something, and spoke in low tones.

Tourists, for sure, I thought.

Dr. Marvel sat with a grim expression on his face, his bony hands clutching the handle of his ancient-looking briefcase. He stared straight ahead.

"What's in your briefcase, Dr. Marvel?"

"Not much."

He popped the clasps open and pulled out a hand-held cassette recorder. Except for a notepad, two pens, and a dog-eared map of the north island, there was nothing else.

"What's that for?" I asked, pointing to the recorder.

"To record the conversation, Meg. Heaven knows, in all the excitement—and I'm sure there's going to be lots of that—I'm likely to miss half the vital information."

Until that moment, I had not allowed myself to become too excited at the thought of meeting two aliens at Te Papa. But now that Dr. Marvel had started talking about it, I felt my anxieties bubbling like lava. I began questioning myself. What was I doing? What was I allowing myself to get into? What if I was abducted?

Oh shut up, Michelle. What can go wrong? You're with Dr. Marvel, aren't you? Yeah, right. Everyone knows he's as nutty as a jar of crunchy peanut butter. Even so, he's kind and—

"What's wrong, child?" I heard Dr. Marvel ask.

"Ummm … nothing."

I took side-long glances at the two men across from us. My thoughts and imaginations became active again. What if they were—

I half-heard Dr. Marvel talking to me in a low whisper.

"They could be tall, short, fat, skinny, old, young … who knows?" he continued. "We must be alert. We must be sure to maintain eye contact with them. To do otherwise might result in us becoming—Molly, are you paying attention?"

Dr. Marvel's elbow jabbed my arm.

"Is your hearing impaired, child?"

"I … yes … no, Dr. M. You were saying something about eyes."

The man came to collect our tickets. I fished my money from my jeans pocket.

"One senior and a child," said Dr. Marvel.

"Ten dollars, sir," replied the man.

Dr. Marvel handed the man twenty dollars, and gently pushed my proffered hand with my five-dollar note, aside. The man handed Dr. Marvel two tickets and some change. With a smile and a wink at me, he walked over to the other two passengers.

"What were you saying about eyes, Dr. M?"

"Nothing …"

The ferry veered to the right, heading for Somes Island. I stared at the isolated rock in the middle of the harbor.

"Somes would have been a better place for our friends to hide instead of at the museum," I whispered to Dr. Marvel.

His bushy eyebrows popped up. "Somes? Why? Which of the inhabitants could they occupy? Sheep? Birds?"

I chuckled. It would be impossible to communicate with either.

The two burly passengers, carrying backpacks and wearing hiking boots, disembarked. One of them stopped, stared right at me, furrowed his brows and scratched his head.

I sucked in my breath as an uneasy feeling swept over me. What if he was Boraz!

"MAF employees—Ministry of Agriculture and Forestry," said Dr. Marvel squaring his shoulders and pushing out his chest.

"How d'you know?" I asked with hesitation.

"See the decals on their backpacks and jackets?"

I relaxed a bit and watched the offloading of several cardboard boxes and other paraphernalia.

About ten minutes later, we sailed away from Somes.

"It was upon that isolated island that unwanted aliens were once quarantined," I heard Dr. Marvel say.

"What? Did you say aliens?" I craned my neck to look at the two men who had disembarked. "Then those two must have been them, Dr. M."

"Them?" Dr. Marvel raised one eyebrow. "Oh, them! No child, those two were not the pair with whom we aim to have our tête-à-tête. No, Somes in days gone by was a place of intrigue of the human kind—not extraterrestrials."

"Oh!" I hoped Dr. Marvel was right.

A rough ride across the harbor might have distracted my thoughts, but today the water was calm; it was like gliding along on ice. Only when the Lynx inter-island ferry zipped past us, did we experience some turbulence. That was more fun, but it didn't last long. I hoped the wind would pick up for our return crossing.

After disembarking at Queens Wharf, we marched at a steady pace along the docks in the direction of Te Papa, paying little attention to the bustle around us. Kids and adults on roller-blades zipped past. I wished I had brought mine.

"Blinking nuisance," said Dr. Marvel under his breath, and jumped aside as a boy about my age almost ploughed into him. "Those things should be banned, or the owners forced to pass a test and wear proper license plates."

The next instant, Dr. Marvel artfully dodged a young blonde roller-blader.

"Did you see that? I almost bowled a maiden over, as they say in cricket," he chuckled.

By now we were walking past the Circa theatre. Te Papa loomed ahead. Dr. Marvel drew to a halt.

"Young Michelle, did you know this entire area was once submerged under water? These massive buildings and walkways are built on land that was reclaimed, following the 1855 earthquake. When the next 'big one' occurs, I shudder to think what might happen."

It was odd hearing Dr. Marvel calmly discussing reclaimed land and earthquakes, when I was having difficulty controlling my breathing and heartbeat. Meeting live aliens was not like going to a movie.

"Are you nervous, Dr. Marvel?" I asked.

Dr. Marvel cleared his throat and resumed walking. "I suppose I am. Aren't you?"

I reached out and took his free hand; it was as cold as mine!

"Yes." I looked up at him. "But we have each other, right?"

He smiled and squeezed my hand.

I was beginning to see a caring, gentle side to Dr. Marvel. Too bad others dismissed him as eccentric and unsociable. It was their loss for not taking the time to get to know him.

Eighteen
Rendezvous with Boraz and Arkon

The massive, irregular concrete structure of Te Papa loomed ahead of us. A large banner hung across one of the advertising spaces at the end of the building.

"Look, Dr. M, the Star Trek exhibit is here. I love Star Trek, especially Spock. Do you watch any of the re-runs?"

"I'm afraid I can't share your enthusiasm, young Molly."

"But the exhibit's only here for a short time. Can't we check it out while we're here? Pleeeease, Dr. M?"

"We must maintain the course we have set ourselves, Millie-girl, or rather, that has been set for us, by those desperate time travelers … er … Borkon and Araz."

"Boraz and Arkon. But you're right, Dr. M, perhaps another time."

We passed together through one quadrant of the huge revolving door.

"Now, what do we do?" I said. "We can't just go up to the information desk and ask for them."

"Indeed not, child. But Bork … I mean Boraz … did say he would find us. Let's wait and see."

I spent the next few minutes staring at people in the hope that one of them might be Boraz. I noticed a man leaning against the wall, near the doorway of the museum shop. He was wearing a crumpled tan trench coat, and a brown fedora hat with the brim pulled down over his dark glasses. The Dominion newspaper he was reading concealed the lower part of his face. His socked feet were jammed into a pair of worn-out sandals.

He had to be one of the aliens, I thought, tugging on Dr. Marvel's arm to draw his attention.

Dr. Marvel did not respond. His eyes were fixed on a security guard standing near the entrance to the Food Train cafeteria.

The guard came shuffling towards us.

"I think that might be one of them," Dr. Marvel whispered.

"What makes you think that?"

"Look at the way he walks, Millie-girl. Platypus feet are not adaptable to human footwear."

As he came closer, the security guard forced his lips into a smile.

"Detective Mitch Jones," he said, holding out his left hand.

I sucked in my breath. How did he know my name? Was something wrong with his right arm?

I stuck my right hand out.

"How do you do?" he said, shaking my hand awkwardly.

"I … I'm fine, thank you. Have we met before?" I said with hesitation, not wanting to risk making a fool of myself.

He took a quick look around; then leaned close to my ear.

"It's me, Boraz."

"Boraz," I repeated. "It's Boraz, Dr. M." I tried to stifle my excitement. "And is that man over there Arkon?" I point over my shoulder.

"What man?" said Boraz.

"The one in the trench coat—reading the newspaper …" I looked over my shoulder. "Oh, he's gone."

Boraz cleared his throat.

"Arkon awaits us at a table in the cafeteria."

His smile was lopsided, as if he was still trying to get used to controlling a human face.

"So, where did you get the bodies?" said Dr. Marvel.

"We've borrowed them from two of the security guards here."

"You did what?" I choked out.

"Don't worry, detective. We're sharing their bodies and minds, but we're in control. When we're ready to leave, they will be returned to normal, with no ill effects."

"What have you done with them, then? I mean, their minds," I asked. "You didn't store them in a bottle or something?"

"No. We've only suppressed them. They won't be harmed."

I was wondering whether they had altered the physical shape and appearance of the borrowed bodies.

"Not really," answered Boraz, reading my mind. "They might just look more radiant than usual, but that's all. Well, almost all. We can't seem to get the hang of walking in this awful Earth footwear."

Boraz pulled a face.

We reached the table, where another security guard was jiggling his ear with his right index finger.

"Arkon ... our guests," said Boraz.

Arkon jumped up, rubbed his finger against the side of his pants, and stuck out his left hand.

"There's something you two have got to get right," I said. "You have to offer your *right* hand if you want to shake hands. Like this."

I extended my right hand, but they just stared, not understanding.

"Stick out your right hand—the one you had in your ear," I whispered.

"Ah, yes," said Arkon, comprehending at last.

We shook hands in the normal way; then he shook Dr. Marvel's hand with much more vigor than he had mine.

"So, these bodies you've occupied, do they have names of their own?" said Dr. Marvel, pulling his hand free.

"I'm Bernie, and he's Chico," said Boraz, jabbing his chest with his thumb and pointed his index finger at Arkon.

"He's Bernie, and I'm Chico," said Arkon at the same time.

Dr. Marvel cleared his throat. "Good, we've got it ... Bernie ... and Chico."

"Hey, guys, do you know Frank?" I asked, hoping either one might know something about the missing security guard Mr. Ihaka had mention to my dad.

"Frank? Frank about what?" asked Dr. Marvel.

"As in being outspoken ... frank?" said Arkon.

"Never mind," I said.

For a couple of minutes after we sat down, no one spoke. Arkon kept shrugging his shoulders and twitching his head to one side. I guessed he was uncomfortable in "his" body. Boraz, on the other hand, kept drumming his fingers on the table and shaking his right leg.

"Are you guys going to say something?" I looked at Arkon and Boraz. "You look so nervous. Is it okay for you two to fraternize with patrons?"

Arkon and Boraz looked at me as if I had spoken in Swahili.

"Which word didn't you understand?" I said.

"This is our sustenance break, detective," said Arkon, scratching his throat.

"Are you hungry? Would you like a mite to eat?" asked Boraz.

Dr. Marvel's eyebrow arched.

"Bite—it's bite to eat—but no thanks, we're fine," he answered. Then, out the side of his mouth, he said to me, "If these two are going to keep mixing up their words, who knows what they might bring us if we asked for a hot dog?"

He was staring through the window at a Scottish terrier basking in the sunshine with its owner.

He cleared his throat. "I'd rather we got on with this … er … whatever it is we're here for, boys."

Dr. Marvel flipped open his briefcase and pulled out his cassette recorder.

"What's that?" said Arkon, staring at the recorder as if it were a hand grenade.

"It's a voice recorder. I'll be recording everything you say," said Dr. Marvel. "That way we'll remember your instructions, in detail."

Boraz and Arkon looked doubtful.

"Don't worry it's only for our benefit. Is that all right?" said Dr. Marvel.

Both men nodded.

"Good as goldfish," said Arkon.

"Gold … good as gold," I said.

Dr. Marvel depressed the "record and play" buttons.

"Right, why did you ask us here?" he asked.

"Did you read the book we left each of you?" asked Boraz.

"I started to … but …" I said

"And mine, as you know, disintegrated before I really had—" began Dr. Marvel.

"Well, I'll feed the contents to you in a crabshell," said Boraz.

"Nutshell," said Dr. Marvel.

From the way the little muscle pulsed at the side of his jaw, I knew he was becoming impatient, wishing these two aliens would get their expressions right.

"Nutshell, crabshell—you get the picture," said Boraz, leaning his elbows on the table. "You, no doubt, have read at least the first chapter of the book we left for each of you, right?"

Dr. Marvel and I nodded.

"Good. Well Arkon and I are those two scientists from Planet Zorb. We developed the S1M1 unit. It is vital for the survival of our people. We had to escape from our planet to conceal it from our archenemy, Saja."

"Somehow, Saja found out about our plans," Arkon continued. "Before we were able to travel to Earth with the unit, he was on our trail. We altered course, hoping to lose him, and when we thought we had, we followed your beam of light."

"You did?" Dr. Marvel looked surprised. "Why didn't you make use of my abode to hide your invention?"

Boraz laughed. "You turned off the beam just as we neared Earth, so we ended up here, at Te Papa. It was not difficult for us to penetrate the concrete walls. Arkon and I agreed this enormous storehouse would be the perfect place to conceal the unit. We hid it among other objects of similar shape."

"The Star Trek exhibits?" I asked.

Arkon's eyes narrowed. "Yes," he said.

I was stunned. "But—"

"What does this S1M1 unit look like?" said Dr. Marvel.

"It's quite similar in size and shape to what you Earth people call a laptop computer," said Arkon.

My antenna shot up.

"A laptop?" I said. Mr. Ihaka had reported a stolen laptop—the SIP! Was there a connection here, or was it just coincidence?

"Can you show it to us?" said Dr. Marvel.

Boraz shook his head. "That's the problem. It's gone … disappeared. We suspect Saja has somehow found it and is at this moment trying to coerce someone into reprogramming it. Our fear is, if Saja's taken possession of the unit, he will use it to alter the minds of our people to suit his needs. That would be a disaster.

"While we occupy human bodies, we cannot make contact with Saja, or he with us. But in our natural state, we are unable to sustain our energy field for long periods of time, when we are outside our native environment."

"That's our dilemma," said Arkon.

While they were talking, my mind was busy sorting out details and coming up with endless questions. Both these aliens and Mr. Ihaka had described a machine that was vital to their people. Were they describing the same thing?

I'd better be careful with my questioning from here on, I thought.

"How come you didn't set off the alarms when you entered Te Papa?" I asked.

Boraz leaned his elbows on the table. "In our natural state, we would have no effect on Earth's security alarms."

"You say this S1M1 holds the collective intelligence of your people," said Dr. Marvel. "What exactly do you mean?"

"The minds of our people are stored in the unit to preserve and protect their knowledge from Saja's evil intent," said Arkon.

"So what has become of your people?" said Dr. Marvel.

"They're mindless and devoid of knowledge at present, for their own protection," said Arkon.

"How would you restore their minds and knowledge?" asked Dr. Marvel.

"That's where you come in. Find the S1M1, and we'll direct the reprogramming. If you don't find it, our people's minds and knowledge may be lost forever," said Boraz.

"I'm an inventor. Make use of my mind by all means, though I must warn you that at times it may be a bit jumbled in there ... but computers, well I don't know much about those crazy machines, which supply answers before you have a chance to think." Dr. Marvel said with haste.

"And I'm not exactly a computer whiz," I said, "but I'm curious about something. Our computers have a CPU—Central Processing unit. It's the part that processes information—the electronic brain. Does this unit of yours have anything similar?"

"The S1M1 is such a unit. You can think of it as a Superior Intelligence Protector ... of minds and knowledge," said Boraz.

"S-I-P!" I whispered, sucking in my breath. My thoughts began to race like a terrier chasing a cat.

So the SIP and the S1M1 are one, and the same. The question is who to believe.... Ihaka? Or these two? What if one of them is really Saja, but pretending to be Boraz or Arkon? Then again, what if Saja is occupying Mr. Ihaka's body?

Fiddlesticks! I have to conceal this knowledge until I could be certain whose side these two aliens were on!

"Spit it out, Michelle, whatever it is you're trying to reason," said Boraz.

His voice was like a thunderbolt in my head and his stare penetrating. The more I fought to control my thoughts, the more compelled I felt to speak.

"Michelle," said Arkon, drawing his eyebrows together. "Cough it out. You'll feel better. Trust me."

Yeah, right. Trust you? I don't think so.

I tightened my lips, struggling against gravity to keep my lower lip pressed against my top lip. As if under a spell, my lips began to separate.

"Look, a man from Te Papa came to see my father a few days ago because he wanted him to investigate the disappearance of something called the SIP—Superior Intelligence Protector … your S1M1 unit—"

"What?" said Arkon, jumping to his feet. "What—?"

"You never told me this," interrupted Dr. Marvel.

"Sorry, Dr. M, but I didn't think it was important."

A lot of heavy breathing followed.

Dr. Marvel opened and closed his mouth, without uttering a single syllable.

Arkon slouched in his chair and combed his fingers through his hair.

I took a deep breath to pull my thoughts together.

Boraz kept nodding his head, as if he was calculating numbers.

"Are you sure about this, detective?" he said in a calm, controlled voice.

"The man told my father someone had broken into Te Papa and stolen the machine. That's all I know. Oh, he also said that once he had the machine, he would take it to his people, who lived in Spapa Stoo Stows."

"Spapa Stoo Stows?" said Dr. Marvel, raising one eyebrow.

"Yeah. He said it was some place in New Zealand, only I couldn't find it on the map. Do you know where that is, Dr. M?" I asked

He furrowed his brow. "You sure you didn't hear him say Papatoetoe?"

I tilted my head to one side. "Nope. He said Spapa Stoo Stows. I'm dead sure."

Dr. Marvel laughed then, and started scribbling on a napkin.

"The way these two have been muddling up their words, I bet my life that what you heard him say was Papatoetoe. It's a Maori word. Don't you see, Papa-toe-toe."

Dr. Marvel broke the word down in syllables.

"Papa Two Toes. See? That's what you heard. There's a place near Auckland by that name," said Dr. Marvel, fishing out the dog-eared map from his briefcase, and spreading it across the table.

With his knobbly index finger, he pointed out the small town.

"That's where you chaps need to be if you plan on ever finding your brain machine," he said, tapping the spot with his finger.

"Papa Two Toes, of course," I said with a nervous laugh. "You're clever to come up with that deduction, Dr. M."

Being Maori, Mr. Ihaka should have known how to pronounce it, I thought.

"Brilliant extraction, Dr. Marvel," remarked Arkon, pulling the map close for a better look. "But I believe the SIP, as you call it, is still here in the Capital." He looked tense.

"Can you describe the man who came to see your father, detective?" said Boraz, his brows furrowed. A muscle pulsed at his temples.

"Well he was short, fat, and walked funny … like his shoes were too tight …" my voice trailed.

"You've described the head of security here at Te Papa," said Arkon. "We've only met him briefly. His name is Harry Ihaka."

My eyes widened.

There was a pause before Boraz spoke.

"Could that be the body Saja's using?" he asked.

"No way, it can't be!" I was emphatic, still uncertain whether to trust these two. "Mr. Ihaka was the one who came to my dad for help. If he were this Saja person, why would he ask my dad to find a machine he already has? It doesn't make any sense. There's no way Saja can be occupying Mr. Ihaka's body."

Boraz drummed his fist on the table. "If Saja is Ihaka, and he hasn't stolen the S1M1, then who has, detective? Tell me."

Maybe you have!

Something else nagged at the back of my mind. The twins had said that a short fat man wearing tight shoes had chased them while they were spying on Professor Grimm. Who was he?

Could that have been Saja? Was he using Professor Grimm to reprogram the SIP?

Questions! So many puzzling ones!

"Now what are you chewing over, detective?" said Boraz, his voice soft but compelling.

"Nothing …"

I looked at Dr. Marvel, but he had a distant look in his eyes.

I began to feel uneasy as another thought rushed into my head. *S-curiosity s-kills the s-cat.* Like Boraz and Arkon, Mr. Ihaka had speech problems. Perhaps Saja *was* masquerading as Mr. Ihaka.

"Dr. Marvel," I said close to his ear. "Do you remember the twins describing the man who chased them?"

"Yeah," he said in his Texan drawl. "What of it?"

"Well, that sounded like a good description of Mr. Ihaka?" I whispered.

Dr. Marvel looked at me with doubtful eyes.

"But why would he be visiting Grimm?" he asked. "No child, I don't believe those two could be in cahoots."

"But, Dr. M—"

"It's preposterous, I say … preposterous."

Dr. Marvel slapped the tabletop. It sounded like a blast from a shotgun. A woman passing with her two young children, jumped, and the younger boy scampered behind his mother's skirt. She looked at us with a frown and hurried her children out of the building.

We must have seemed a strange group!

I was glad Dr. Marvel didn't accept my theory, though. My dad wouldn't help anyone who was on the side of evil.

"Yeah, you're right, Dr. M. It must have been someone else."

Like these two.

I stared at Boraz, determined not to blink, and even more determined to conceal my thoughts.

"What's preposterous, Dr. Marvel?" he said. "And there is something else you're not telling us, young detective. What is it?"

I chewed on my bottom lip. I wasn't going to say anything more about Mr. Ihaka. After all, he was my father's client.

Boraz's eyes bore into mine.

I looked away.

"Look, Michelle, we recruited you as our detective. If you have vital information, we want it. Tell us again about Ihaka seeking your father's help. Spill your thoughts this instant," said Boraz's, his voice smooth but insistent.

I interlaced my fingers, not daring to look up.

"I've already said too much. Dad would be angry if he knew I was discussing his client with complete strangers," I said in a weak voice. My throat felt parched.

Boraz sighed. "But we're not strangers, are we, Michelle?"

His tone was sincere, but my mind was confused.

"Look, Millie-girl, if we're to help these gentlemen, you've got to cooperate," said Dr. Marvel leaning one elbow on the table, and jabbing the air with the index finger of his other hand. "The important thing we have to remember here is …" He paused; his index finger remained motionless as if frozen in midair.

"The important thing is what?" I pulled at Dr. Marvel's coat sleeve, half-hoping he, too, had some doubts about Boraz and Arkon.

Dr. Marvel turned his head with deliberate slowness, his eyes fixed on my face.

"Yes, yes … the important thing is … I need a cup of American coffee—black."

It was just like Dr. Marvel to bail me out of a tricky situation. I jumped up, glad for the diversion.

"Thanks, Dr. M," I whispered in his ear; then aloud, "One black American coffee coming right up. Boraz? Arkon? Do you want anything to drink?"

They both declined.

I dashed to the coffee counter.

Please, God, I prayed, *don't let them force me to tell any more.*

I felt a strong temptation to flee from Te Papa and catch the first available ferry back to the protection of home, and Dad.

Nineteen
How Many Know?

I returned with Dr. Marvel's coffee and a hot chocolate for me.

"Just the stimulant required," he said, taking a long swallow. He smacked his lips then leaned back in his chair. His eyes fastened on me. "To begin at the beginning is essential before the end can be achieved." He swirled his coffee cup, then drained it with loud gulps.

"Would you like another coffee, Dr. M?" I said.

"Tell your tale from the beginning, Millie-girl?" he said. "Tell us about this Ihaka chap. I'll then have a candid picture of the beginning, and so, eventually, the end."

I felt betrayed. Dr. Marvel wasn't on my side after all.

I buried my lips in the brown chocolate froth threatening to flow over the side of my cup. I could feel three sets of eyes boring into me, compelling me to speak. I felt trapped and afraid. Tiny beads of sweat formed on my forehead.

"Don't be afraid, Michelle," said Boraz, reaching across the table and taking my free hand in his. "Please … it's just that we don't have much time left to save our people."

There was a sense of urgency in his grasp.

With some reservations, I told them everything I knew about Mr. Ihaka. I didn't tell them I'd broken into my father's office and listened to the recording, but I did tell them that the twins and I had planned to investigate the Te Papa robbery by ourselves.

"What?" said Boraz. His right shoulder began to twitch. "Have you dared to involve others? Who are these twins? Can they be trusted?"

"Pull your horns in, Boraz. Dr. Marvel has them bound under a secrecy wristband. While they're bound, they won't remember anything about you, or the SIP. That is, until Dr. Marvel releases them."

"Ah," said Boraz, "I see."

The twitching stopped.

"A secrecy wristband would be useful to us, Boraz," said Arkon.

"Indeed it would," said Boraz. "We might be able to use it to control Saja's rebels, once we return to our planet."

"I'll consider the request after I've pondered it's relevance to your cause," said Dr. Marvel. "For now, let's just concentrate on our search for the SIP, shall we?"

We lapsed into silence.

Privately, I was busy trying to work out my dilemma. I wished I had not been so forthcoming with information. I wished I had some kind of truth serum to use on these two. Who should I trust? Mr. Ihaka, Professor Grimm? Boraz? Arkon? I would pretend to trust Boraz, while observing his body language.

I took a deep breath, determined to sound genuinely concerned. "Boraz, if Saja is occupying Mr. Ihaka's body, do you think he is counting on my father to find the SIP? And do you believe Saja has already recruited Professor Grimm to reprogram it?"

Boraz cupped his hand under his chin, his bushy eyebrows bunched up in a frown. He made no eye contact when he answered.

"That may well be, of course, detective," he said. "Except we don't know for sure if Saja has assumed a human body, and whether that body happens to be Ihaka's."

"But if he is using Mr. Ihaka's body—"

"If that is true," interrupted Arkon, "someone has to keep an eye on your father to make sure he doesn't just hand over the S1M1 … the SIP, to Ihaka."

Boraz cleared his throat. "Will you agree to do it, detective?"

This time he looked at me.

I blinked. I hadn't expected this request. "That's not going to be easy. "My father strictly forbade me to get involved in this particular case. Besides if he does find the SIP how can I stop him from handing it over to Mr. Ihaka? Have you considered that someone else might already know where the SIP is?"

Boraz and Arkon pinned pleading eyes on me.

"Look, my father received a phone call from someone—a man. He said he had information about who stole the SIP. He would only tell my father if he agreed to pay for the info. Maybe *that man* has it."

Boraz leaned forward, suddenly more alert. "Someone else beside the four of us, your father, Saja, Grimm, and the twins know about the SIP? I can't believe this. Who is he?"

"I don't know." My mouth felt dry. I had difficulty swallowing.

"How come you didn't tell me about this other chap, young Margaret?" Frown lines creased Dr. Marvel's forehead, and a vein pulsed at his temple.

"I didn't remember until now, Dr. M."

"Did he make any peculiar sounds to indicate his breed?" said Dr. Marvel.

"I'm pretty sure he wasn't a dog—"

"Ethnic origin, child ... accent ..."

"Can't say for sure, Dr. M. He might have been holding a hanky or something over the mouthpiece."

"I don't like the sound of this," said Boraz. "I can't imagine who else would be involved."

"Don't you see? If the man said he knew who stole the SIP then it can't possibly be Mr. Ihaka who did the deed, can it?" I tried to reason.

The situation was about as clear as mud to me, but at least, I wouldn't need to spy on my father.

"Then whose body is Saja occupying?" said Boraz in a resigned voice.

"Drat!" said Arkon. "We're no further ahead, are we? We're going around in cycles."

Dr. Marvel scratched his head. "Cycles, squares, oblongs—whatever the shape, this business is getting far too complicated—too many variables. Perhaps we should just let the good detective what's-his-name do his job."

"Jones," I said. "Jones, PI, senior."

"No! The senior detective must not be told about us," said Arkon. "We don't want any of this getting back to Saja, you understand."

There was a long pause before Boraz spoke again.

"We tried to make contact with you on Thursday night, detective, when you were asleep. Two days ago, I tried sending you a help message on your computer. I even tried to tell you about Zorb through your assignment. Had you been more alert, we might not have lost the SIP in the first place."

"I ... I ... sorry!" My voice was barely above a whisper. I studied Boraz's face, looking for any signs of insincerity. There was none!

"You kept calling me 'moron'. What's a 'moron'?" he asked.

I looked up and saw the man with the fedora hat and tan trench coat, newspaper rolled under his right armpit, walking towards our table. My mouth opened and shut. Before I had a chance to warn the others of his approach, he spoke.

"Michelle! Dr. Marvel!" His mouth was tight and grim.

My heart skipped several beats. "Dad! What are you doing here, dressed like a bum?"

Stupid question!

Dad's eyes and stern face spoke volumes. "Call it intuition, Michelle. I thought you two were supposed to be looking at planets."

Dad stared at Boraz and Arkon, one eyebrow raised. "How come you're talking to security? Got her into trouble no doubt, eh Marvel?" Dad's eyes blazed.

Dr. Marvel cleared his throat, ignoring Dad's accusing eyes and tone.

"Ah, Detective Jones senior, as in not junior," he began with deceptive calm. "You shouldn't jump to such preposterous conclusions. What could be amiss in a public setting such as this? Why, these two gentlemen were kind enough to inform us that the planetary display was dismantled for relocation to another floor. So, it seems our mission here has been a total waste of time. And since it was their hour of nourishment, they invited us to partake, before we departed on the floating vessel that brought us."

"Eh?" said Dad.

He surveyed the table before resting his eyes on my hot chocolate and Dr. Marvel's empty coffee cup. He shook his head and I knew he didn't believe Dr. Marvel's diatribe.

"I'm heading back home now and you two are coming with me," said Dad.

"We are?" I looked at Dr. Marvel.

"Ah, yes, a splendid idea," he said. "Our business here is at an impasse." He scrambled to his feet. "Thank you, gentlemen, for your assistance. Since the reassembly of the display will not commence anytime soon, we'd best be off."

"Display? What display?" asked Arkon.

Dr. Marvel cleared his throat. "The solar system ... what young Michelle here needs to finish her science project. When did you say it was due, child?"

"Mon ... Monday ... er ... tomorrow," I squeaked.

"I'd say you're in deep trouble," said Dad, raising one eyebrow.

A smile played at the corner of his mouth and I had a feeling he didn't believe me, or Dr. Marvel for that matter. How could he? There was no way I could complete a science project by tomorrow if I had to rely on Te Papa's galactic display.

"Come on Michelle, Dr. Marvel, let's go." Dad tipped his hat at Boraz and Arkon. He marched off, slipping off his trench coat, and draping it over his arm.

"We haven't finished our purpose here," I heard Boraz whisper to Dr. Marvel.

I heard Dr. Marvel clear his throat. When I looked back, he was pulling a business card from his breast pocket.

"Make use of this," I heard him say, handing the card to Boraz.

I saw Boraz reach for the card. Their knuckles banged together and almost immediately a beam of blue light shot out of Boraz's right ear, and disappeared into Dr. Marvel's left ear. There was a grimace on Dr. Marvel's face. I opened and shut my mouth, suddenly feeling afraid for Dr. Marvel. But with a shake of his head, he was himself again. I breathed a sigh of relief.

"Before darkness gives way to dawn, two sparrows will nest before rest. We will again meet," said Boraz.

"Aloha," said Dr. Marvel, charging after me.

"You didn't believe them, did you, Dr. M?"

"I must remain silent on that for now, Millie-girl."

We spoke in low tones.

"And what did Boraz mean about sparrows needing rest?"

"I must remain silent on that, too, child."

"What do we do next, then?" I asked.

"Investigate Grimm," said Dr. Marvel.

"But you said he couldn't be involved—"

"Changed my mind."

"So when, Dr. M? When do we investigate?"

"When the sun lies down to sleep."

"Say what—?"

Dad looked over his shoulder at us and raised one eyebrow. I knew his investigative mind was telling him there was more going on with Dr. Marvel, the security guards, and me. How I wished I could tell him everything—but what good would that do? I still wasn't sure who the bad guys were.

Twenty
Dad's Agenda

I climbed into the back seat. Dr. Marvel sat erect and tight-lipped in the front seat, his briefcase cradled against his chest. We drove away from the museum in silence. Dad headed for Vivian Street, as if we were going home, but, instead of turning onto the motorway, he flew past and swung right, onto The Terrace.

"Are we going to the university to see Mom?"

Dad turned left onto Salamanca Road. He looked at me in the rear-view mirror and smiled. I knew he was up to something. When he pulled into the upper end of the Botanic Gardens, I sucked in my breath.

"Why are we here, Dad?"

"You need to research that *tenth* planet for your project, don't you? This is where the Carter Observatory is."

"But …?" I chewed on my top lip.

Think, Michelle, think. You have to get out of this.

Dr. Marvel cleared his throat. "We have been whacking the sheep with its missing tail, young Meg." He looked over his shoulder at me. "The Observatory is just the place to observe that new planet."

"It is?"

"The sky's at our disposal. We must grasp it with both hands, child."

"But, Dr. M, what chance do we have of observing planets at this time of day? It's only three. It's bright and sunny, and—"

"You may not be able to view astronomical phenomena with the naked eye, Michelle, but they have powerful telescopes in there, don't they, Dr. Marvel?" said Dad.

"Quite so, detective … er … Holmes," he replied.

98

Dr. Marvel climbed out of the Land Rover and hurried up the path to the Carter Observatory. I followed meekly, with Dad bringing up the rear.

"For someone on the brink of disaster with your school project, you're not too enthusiastic about researching this so-called tenth planet, are you, Fifi?" said Dad.

I pretended not to hear. Instead, I walked a little faster to keep ahead of him.

By now, Dr. Marvel had reached the main doors to the Observatory. He made a good show of trying to pull them open. He turned and shrugged his shoulders.

"What's wrong, Dr. M?" I asked.

"I'm afraid we've wasted our time again," he replied. "Public viewing of planets, dead or alive, is on Tuesday evenings between the hours of 7.30 and 9.30."

I sighed. "Oh, that's too bad."

"Two strikes, eh?" said Dad. "That's a shame, Fifi."

A smile played at the corner of his mouth. Maybe he had known all along that the Observatory was closed; he had just wanted to see my reaction.

Our drive home was uneventful. Dr. Marvel and I had no further chance to discuss our next move, with Dad present. When Dad tried to engage Dr. Marvel in conversation about the teething problems with the newest inter-island ferry, his response was vague and unenthusiastic. Dr. Marvel had a habit of switching off when things didn't interest him or when he had other things on his mind.

It was almost four-thirty when we stopped in front of Dr. Marvel's driveway. When he did not attempt to leave the Land Rover, Dad leaned over and opened the door.

"We're here, Dr. Marvel," he said.

"Here? Here where?" said Dr. Marvel, staring straight ahead, his breathing raspy.

"Is something wrong, Dr. M?" I asked.

Dr. Marvel's face was turning pink and droplets of sweat dripped from his chin.

"What's wrong must be put right." Dr. Marvel mopped his face with his sleeve. "And it will." He snapped his head forward and looked towards his house. "I'm home?"

Dad cleared his throat. "That's what I've been trying to tell you."

"Then why didn't you say so in concise English, young man." Dr. Marvel grabbed his briefcase and jumping out. Without a backward glance, he scampered up his driveway.

Dad released a long, slow whistle. "I swear that man has a lot more dead brain cells than there are hairs on his head. And you think he can help with your science project?"

I shrugged my shoulders. "Well, I guess we'll never know, Dad."

Poor Dr. M! I knew he was burdened with other matters. Our meeting with Boraz and Arkon had created more questions than answers.

"Have you saved your project on disc?" Dad asked.

"Yes. Why?"

"I'll help you with it tonight, okay. We'll surf the net for information on your tenth planet. How's that?"

"But Dad—"

"No *buts*, Michelle. I'll help you. That way you won't have to bother Looney Tunes anymore. Besides, you did say your assignment was due tomorrow, didn't you?"

"Yes, Dad." I laced my fingers together. Telling lies like this was eating away at my insides. "Dad …!"

"What?"

"Nothing."

Twenty-One
Missing Again!

As soon as we reached home, I dashed to the phone and dialed Dr. Marvel's number. I needed to know if he was all right, and whether he had developed a plan to spy on Professor Grimm. His phone was busy. I dialed the twins' number. Mrs. Owen answered.

"Hello, Mrs. Owen, it's Michelle. May I speak to Robert, please?"

"Hello dear, I'm sorry, but the boys aren't here. Aren't they over there?"

Why would Mrs. Owen think they are over here?

My brain went into overdrive.

Where can they be? Blast! What are they up to now?

"Hello?" Mrs. Owen's voice penetrated my thoughts. "Well, are the boys over there?"

"Oh, they must be playing computer games with my brother. Thanks, Mrs. Owen. Bye."

I hung up before she could say anything else. I turned, intending to dash out the front door, but ran smack into Dad's broad chest.

"Was that Mom? I didn't hear the phone," he said.

"No … it was Mrs. Owen … I called her."

"Why?"

"To speak to the twins, but they're out."

Dad's right eyebrow raised a fraction. With little time to think, I raced to my room, leaving him staring after me.

My mind was in a whirl. I needed to focus. Maybe the twins were at Dr. Marvel's. But suppose I called Dr. Marvel and found they were not there, what then? With Dad around, I would have to be careful with what I said. Dad was too clever to be fooled.

When I heard him going down to his office, I knew he would discover the unlocked desk.

"Trouble, eh?" said Teddy.

"Big time! The twins have disappeared again, and Dad's going to sting me up me for tampering with his desk."

"That's bad, real bad, Mitch PI"

I prayed for divine intervention as I heard Dad's heavy footsteps trudging down the hall towards my room.

"This is it, Teddy. I'm going to be grounded for the rest of my natural life."

"Michelle?" Dad poked his head in. "Look, honey, I've got to go out for a while. Tell Jason to fetch some fish and chips for tea."

"Okay, Dad." I couldn't believe he had not yelled at me. Thank you, Lord.

"Get on with your science project. Download whatever you can from the internet. I'll expect to see a copy when I get back. In other words, Michelle, I don't want you out of the house. It's going to get dark soon. Got that?"

"Yes, Dad." But I was thinking about the twins. Where were they?

"Bye, Fifi. See you later. Remember what I said. Don't leave the house ... and I mean that."

I flopped onto the bed, deflated. I heard Dad close the front door. His footsteps hurried down the path. I didn't hear him start the car. Wherever he was going, he was getting there on foot. That bothered me. If I intended to sneak out, I would have to be extra careful not to bump into him. Well, I had to move into action, whatever the consequences. There was no time to pre-plan. I had to find the twins.

I fetched my detective bag from the closet.

"If you're going to disobey your dad, at least wait 'til it gets dark."

"But I don't like being out in the dark, Teddy."

"Well, it ain't gonna be daylight anytime soon, and you ain't gonna find the twins in five minutes."

I raced to the phone and dialed Dr. Marvel's number.

"Hallo!"

Dr. Marvel's yell almost burst my eardrum.

"Hi, Dr. M, it's me." I jiggled my ear with my index finger to clear the temporary blockage.

"Me? Me who? Whatever you're selling, I don't want any. You telemarketers are a pain in the-you-know-where. Go bother someone else, missy."

Oh, no, it sounded like Dr. Marvel was caught up in one of his strange trances again. I should have said goodbye straightaway and waited a while longer for him to return to his normal self, but I didn't. "It's Michelle, Dr. M. What's wrong?"

"Wrong? What could be wrong? The world's my clam … now that they're here."

What did he mean? "Do you mean the twins? Are they with you, Dr. M? That's a relief."

"Twins? I don't see any twins … triplets … or quadruplets. Nope, twins can't be here otherwise I'd be seeing doubles, unless of course they're ghosts. As for relief, try enemas. Is that it? Do you have another puzzle? If you don't, then go away. I'm busy. Oh, hang on, I get it, the only twin I see is when I look into the mirror. Ha! Ha!" He slammed down the receiver.

Boy, Dr. Marvel sure sounded weird. He was talking to me as if I were a total stranger or something.

The twins were not at his house, and right now, that fact was more important than whatever confused mood possessed Dr. Marvel. Even so, I returned to my room, frustrated because I was unable to establish when we were going to spy on Professor Grimm.

The house phone rang. I refused to answer it, in case it was Mrs. Owen. I crossed my fingers hoping Jason would ignore it too. When the answering machine kicked in, I raced to the living room. Mrs. Owen's voice was asking Mom if she would mind keeping the twins overnight because she and Mr. Owen were going out to a dinner party. A blessing in disguise, I thought, erasing the message.

Curious as to why Jason hadn't answered the phone, I looked in his room. He was fast asleep on his bed, mouth agape, an open textbook hanging half off his chest. If I knew my brother, he would sleep for hours. I resisted the temptation to daub some of Mom's makeup on his face. I pulled the door shut.

My only other concern now, was Mom. I dialed her number at work.

"Faculty of English, Dr. Jones speaking—"

"Hi, Mom! When are you coming home?"

"Hello, Michelle, how are you, sweetie? I'll be just a bit late, honey. Will you tell Dad some of my colleagues and I will be going out for tea … I should be home around ten or so."

Excellent! I wasn't about to complain. This was in my favor. Of course, I said nothing about Mrs. Owen's request. The coast was clear … I had to find the twins!

"You'll have to look after your own tea," I heard Mom say, but when I didn't answer straight away, she said, "Michelle …?"

"Heard ya, Mom. Don't worry about us. We'll probably have fish and chips."

"How did your research go?"

"What research?"

"With Dr. Marvel at Te Papa, darling."

"Oh, that! Not so good."

"Sorry to hear that. Look, tell me all about it later. I've got to go."

Mom hung up. My non-existent project was threatening to cause me some embarrassment, but I would worry about it later. Right now, I had other problems to deal with.

I turned on a few lights around the house, before going to my room to prepare. The twins were my priority now. My instincts told me to stake out Professor Grimm's house.

I switched on my bedside radio, before putting on my black detective gear. I scribbled a do-not-disturb note and stuck it with scotch tape to my bedroom door.

Grabbing my detective bag, I tiptoed past Jason's room. I thought of Teddy and rushed back to get him. I stuffed him into my bag. I would need all the help I could get.

I crept into my parent's bedroom and pocketed Dad's skeleton key.

In the hallway, I took Mom's green facemask from my bag and daubed it all over my face. I looked at my reflection in the mirror. The person looking back at me had two dark eyeballs staring out of a green face. Not bad. I would blend into the darkness and the foliage quite well.

I snuck out the front door. The bush path the twins and I had used before would be best. I didn't want to risk bumping into anyone, especially Dad. I would drop by Dr. Marvel to let him know that I was going to stake out Professor Grimm.

Flickering lights from neighboring houses guided my footsteps. It was quiet; the German Shepherd must have been preoccupied with his rubber bone.

Remembering the attacks of the wild rose bushes, I paused to put on Mom's special rosebush gloves. They were a bit loose, but provided the shield I needed against stabbing thorns.

When I reached Dr. Marvel's house, I plopped behind a clump of low shrub, not far from his front steps. Lights were on in his living room and kitchen. Across the lane, the camper-van was still parked in the driveway. I felt chilly, so I pulled Teddy out of my detective bag and hugged him.

"Now what, Teddy?"

"We wait a minute or two."

"We?"

"You and me … us two. Do you see anyone else here?"

Sometimes I had to laugh at myself. You'd think I was having a conversation with a living, breathing person. But, hey, when you're stuck in the dark, you're grateful to talk to anything.

"Is that what I am? Anything?"

"Sssh, Teddy."

My eyes locked onto a man carrying a bulky package. He bounded up Dr. Marvel's front steps and banged on the door.

It opened almost immediately.

"Hallo!" I heard Dr. Marvel say.

"Special delivery," said the man.

"But I'm not expecting one," said Dr. Marvel.

"This is 35 Moa, isn't it?" said the man.

"Ah-ha … yes, yes, so it is. Well, come in, come in. Don't stand out there man."

I heard the door slam shut.

My mind changed gears and slipped into overdrive. Who was this stranger? What was he delivering to Dr. Marvel's at this time on a Sunday evening? A depressing thought occurred to me just then.

What if Dr. M is a double agent? After all, he is a scientist. He could be interested in the SIP for selfish reasons. What if Saja is occupying his body?

"Stop it, Michelle," I whispered. "Dr. Marvel is nuts, but he's not possessed!"

"Don't be too sure of that," said Teddy.

"Stifle that thought, old Bear," I said, stuffing him back into my bag. "I'd better get on with finding those boys."

I felt like a possum scrounging through scrub and bush. The only difference was possums had natural night vision, while I had to work hard at picking my way through the darkness.

I made it to the Ngaio tree in Professor Grimm's backyard. My hands were sweating, so I peeled off Mom's gardening gloves and stuffed them into my detective bag.

Just as I stepped from behind the Ngaio tree, a man walked round the corner of the house. I pulled back. With caution, I allowed one eye to peer around the tree-trunk. My breathing became heavy, and my heart danced as if to the rhythm of African drums. When the man came into full view under the outdoor light, I was shocked. He was the same man who had visited Dr. Marvel less than ten minutes earlier. He was still carrying the same package under his arm.

"Blow! What is this? Delivery night or what? First Dr. Marvel, now Professor Grimm!" I said.

The man stomped up the steps to the back door, but before he could knock, the door flew open.

"What took you so long?" growled the man who had opened the door. It didn't sound like Professor Grimm.

"Look, you want this package, or not?"

"Give it here."

The deliveryman stepped back, lifting the package out of reach.

"You gotta sign for it first, mate," he said.

The man at the door stepped forward under the porch light. It wasn't Professor Grimm, yet he looked familiar. I couldn't see his face, but his shape reminded me of someone I'd seen before.

The deliveryman handed over the package, and the other man retreated into the house. For a moment, I could see into the kitchen. Just before the door closed, I caught a glimpse of Professor Grimm. What were the two of them up to?

I crept forward once more and tiptoed up the steps. With my ear pressed against the door, I could barely make out what the two men were saying.

"Is that it?"

"Yes, Grimm. It's the equipment. Did you cook fish today?"

"No. Why?"

"Well, I smell fish. When it stinks of fish, something's fishy."

"Meaning?" said Professor Grimm.

I heard sniffing sounds.

"Meaning, someone or something is hanging around where it shouldn't."

I had heard those words before, from the twins. They had said that when they were spying on Professor Grimm. The man who chased them had been talking about the smell of fish. I sniffed the air—no fish smell!

Footsteps charging towards the door sent me dashing back to the Ngaio tree. From behind the large trunk, I peered at the backdoor just as it opened. The man came hobbling down the steps in his tight-fitting shoes sniffing like a dog. He headed straight for my tree.

I didn't hang around. Clutching my detective bag, I raced into the bushes intending to make my way back home. I could hear the man's heavy footsteps thumping after me.

THUMP, THUMP, THUMP!

"Run Michelle, move those skinny legs," I whispered.

One mighty tug on my ponytail brought me to a sudden stop. I staggered backwards. My detective bag flew out of my hand.

With my eyes tightly closed, I waited. This was it. I had a premonition of the headlines in tomorrow's newspaper: *Girl detective, Mitch Jones, disappears! Searchers unable to locate body.*

I squeezed my eyes shut, waiting for my pursuer to finish scalping me. Nothing happened. When I tried to look over my shoulder, a searing pain surged through my head bringing instant tears. I was trapped, but there was still fight left in me.

The *thump, thump* sound pounded even louder in my ears. The man was getting closer.

I balled my fist. "Oh no you don't, you mean, nasty, fish-smelling beast ..."

With all my might, I spun around and drove my fist straight at my assailant's mid-section.

"Take that, you ... *ouch*!"

My fist connected with several spiky thorns. "You stupid rosebush," I growled.

"Yo! Mitch, PI!" It was Teddy's voice. "How come you dropped me like a pile of hot potatoes?"

I didn't answer right away because I was busy disengaging the end of my ponytail from the rosebush. That's when I realized that the *thump, thump, thump* sound was my own heart racing like a revved up engine. Now I was mad, crazy mad. Once I had freed my hair, I reached for my detective bag and grabbed the cutters and Mom's old garden gloves.

"Yo! Mitch! Don't tell me you've had a fright. Some stake-out detective you are."

Again, I ignored Teddy's remarks. I marched back to the offending rose bush, and snipped off the branches, which had had the audacity to snag my ponytail.

"That was the last time you're ever going to launch surprise attacks you stupid rose bush."

I returned the cutters to my bag, but kept the gloves on. I braced my back against the trunk of a cabbage tree. Why did the man connect my presence to the smell of fish? I sniffed my armpits. Fresh sweat—not fishy, just pure clean fresh sweat. But I was wearing Jason's old tracksuit!

Except for the occasional hoot of a Morepork searching the woods for its supper, the night was silent. The man must have gone back into the house by now.

I felt compelled to return and find out what was going on at Grimm's House. I removed my nametag and slipped it into the pocket of my detective pants.

Twenty-Two
A Sinister Experiment

I tiptoed up the back steps and pressed my ear against the door. No sounds came from the kitchen. The door did not budge when I turned the knob. I would have to risk breaking in!

I pulled out Dad's skeleton key from my detective bag.

"You just gotta fit, please," I whispered. "I gotta get in there." My heart pulsed.

"You sure you wanna do this?" said Teddy.

"Don't have a choice."

"And the fishy smell?"

"What about it?"

"You just got chased because of it."

"But I don't smell like fish, do I?"

"It's your goose to cook, Mitch PI"

I poked the key into the keyhole of the Yale lock, twisting it firmly.

Click!

The sound sent tingles through my body.

I turned the knob; the door opened!

"Thank you!" I whispered, kissing the key, before slipping it into my pocket.

I pushed the door open just a crack—enough for my eyes to scan the kitchen. No one was there. I eased the door open a bit more, just enough to see into the living room and surrounding areas. Everything was quiet.

Leaving my detective bag outside the door, I slipped into the kitchen. I eased the door shut, after making sure the catch was on the lock, in case I had to make a hasty escape.

A blue and white china bowl piled high with fresh lemons stood on the kitchen table.

Perfect!

Beside the bowl I noticed a shiny, black-handled, paring knife.

Double perfect!

I grabbed the knife and sliced through a medium sized lemon, then squeezed the juice into my palms. I rubbed the juice into my hair, dabbed some on the front of my black detective clothes, and under my armpits.

That should kill any fishy smell.

I tiptoed across the ceramic tiles and headed for the living room. One floor lamp illuminated the room. A pair of orange overalls, with *Department of National Security* printed in large black letters across them, was draped over the back of the sofa.

On the sofa was a hairy mass—perhaps a cat stretched out on a red blanket. I grabbed a magazine from the coffee table and poked it. It didn't move. Dead cat? Closer examination revealed a wig with long brown hair tied back in a ponytail.

The person Dad had met on Friday night had a ponytail!

I grabbed the ponytail and shook it. A small fur-ball dropped to the floor.

A fake moustache!

The red blanket was a red sweater! Reuben's!

My right eye began to twitch. Did that mean trouble? Or was something good going to happen? I could never remember.

A dull thud, followed by a groan from an adjoining room, sent me scrambling for cover behind the sofa. When neither Professor Grimm nor his companion appeared, I breathed easier and slunk away from my hiding place.

A much louder thud startled me. This time, footsteps charging up the steps from the basement made me dive behind the sofa again. I peered out just in time to see Professor Grimm hurrying towards the room the disturbance had come from.

He opened the door and poked his head in.

"It's no good carrying on like that," he said from the doorway.

He slipped a key out of his pocket and locked the door. He left the key in the lock and hurried back down the steps.

I was tempted to investigate the room. I crept towards it.

A whirring sound and whisperings coming from the basement distracted me. I dropped onto my hands and knees and crawled towards the door leading down to the flat.

I could hear voices, probably Professor Grimm and the man who chased me.

I strained to hear what the voices were saying. Curiosity made me creep down the steps. I saw two doors—one wide open, the other slightly ajar. From this latter room, I could hear the soft purring of a machine.

I crept closer and positioned myself where I could hear what the men were saying.

"You know what curiosity did to puss-cat?" Teddy's voice bellowed in my head.

Hush, will you. This is important, I said in my mind.

The two men spoke in low tones.

"How much longer, Grimm? One s-minute? s-Two? Six? What?"

I jiggled my ear with my index finger. That voice sounded like Harry Ihaka's. I wished I had a drinking glass, to do Dr. Marvel's listening trick. I inched closer to the opening.

"I don't have a magic wand, you know. Besides the package arrived late," said Professor Grimm.

"If you had asked s-me, I s-could have brought it s-to you yesterday. So how s-much longer? Surely you s-must have an idea."

"Back off, will you. I said *soon*," replied Professor Grimm.

"Okay, okay! Don't bust your jockstrap. Are the subjects ready?"

"They're all wired up and ready to go. Now shut up. I need to check this one last time," said Professor Grimm.

"Get on with it, then."

"Let me get this straight. The idea here is when we plug this thing in, one of the subjects will become docile and the other violent? Is that right?"

"Affirmative. It's good they're so alike. s-Perfect for our little experiment."

"But why do you insist on doing this at all? Isn't there enough violence in the world?"

"s-Think about it Grimm. If it works, it s-may be a way to deal with the s-prison s-population."

"We should be experimenting on possums."

"And get those animal rights people on our backs? No Grimm, that would be foolish. Besides time is a luxury I don't have. The SIP s-must be one hundred s-percent operational as soon as possible."

The SIP!

I sucked in my breath. That was Harry Ihaka, all right. Could Boraz be right in suspecting the rebel Saja was occupying Mr. Ihaka's body and somehow controlling Professor Grimm as well? They were about to test the SIP on two subjects—two subjects who were alike!

The twins!

My heart sounded like two revved-up rally cars, readying for take off. What should I do? Whatever happened now, I'd have to deal with it alone. There wasn't time to go get Dad or Dr. Marvel.

I could hear soft moans coming from the other room. I crept towards it. An overhead light dimly illuminated the room, but I was able to make out two small figures lying on their backs on single beds separated by a low table.

A laptop computer without a monitor was on the table. Was that the SIP? Cables connected it to the foreheads of the two bodies on the beds.

The sight of the identical blond heads made me gasp. I snuck into the room.

The boys had packaging tape across their mouths. Their wrists were taped together, so too were their ankles.

"What are you two doing here?" I said, kneeling beside one of the beds. The bushy eyebrows revealed that I was talking to Robert. "Those bands were supposed to keep you out of this case."

Robert rolled his eyes.

"Did the professor grab you while you and Reuben were out riding?"

Robert wrinkled his nose and tried to move his lips.

The strong smell of my lemon juice cologne tickled my nose, causing a rapid build-up of air. I pinched the end of my nose to stem its explosive exit, but …

"Aaaachoo!"

It sounded like a blast from a shotgun. Immediately, I heard footsteps racing from the room next door.

Robert's eyes widened and he began to groan and wriggle.

Twenty-Three
Something's Fishy All Right

I dove under Robert's bed, seconds before Grimm and his companion thundered into the room.

"Any more sound effects from either one of you and it's going to be lights out—and I don't s-mean the electric s-kind. Got it?" said a familiar voice.

I was staring at footwear and pant cuffs. The bulging shoes, with shoelaces straining to hold them together, confirmed the presence of Harry Ihaka. What sort of game was the two-faced rat playing? He knew all along where the SIP was, yet he had lied to my father. Why?

"Fish! I smell fish again, and I don't s-mean these two," said Ihaka. I could hear him sniffing.

I held my breath. This was unbelievable. How could he smell fish when all I could smell was lemons?

"What's with you and fish?" said Grimm. "I just smell lemons. I've got a bowl full of 'em on the kitchen table."

"Bah! Can't fool s-me," said Ihaka, standing right in front of my eyes.

I resisted the urge to reach out and tie his shoelaces together. It would have been so satisfying to watch him fall flat on his fat face.

"The smell of fish s-tells me some unwanted thing is prowling s-nearby," said Ihaka.

"Come off it, Harry. Stop the paranoia, for Pete's sake. You and your stupid snout are driving me crazy," said Grimm. "Let's go. We've work to do. These two can't cause much trouble, trussed up like that."

"If you weren't so slow, we'd have finished the s-test by s-now," said Ihaka.

I breathed a sigh of relief when the two pairs of shoes clumped out of the room, pulling the door shut behind them. I counted to twenty before easing myself from under the bed.

"Try not to make a noise," I whispered to the terrified twins. "I've got a good idea what those men are planning. Somehow I've gotta protect your butts, until help arrives."

I had to cross my fingers because I wasn't expecting any help. No one knew where I was, and I wasn't sure Dr. Marvel even remembered we were going to spy on Professor Grimm.

I needed to work fast. I knelt down to unplug the SIP and found a discarded extension cable sitting on the floor behind the desk. This I plugged into the power point on the wall. Removing a lace from one of my running shoes, I tied the two cables together, hoping to give the illusion that the SIP was still connected to the power outlet.

Robert looked like he wanted to tell me something, but I didn't dare remove the tape from his mouth.

"Sssh," I whispered. "Don't try to mumble. They might hear. Everything'll be okay."

I crept over to Reuben and told him the same thing.

The boys kept staring at me. Maybe they hadn't seen me in Jason's tracksuit before, or maybe it was my green face. My mind was in turmoil. I had to get us out of this mess.

"Look Reuben, there isn't much time to explain," I whispered, "but I think they're going to do some testing on you two. One of you must behave violently while the other acts dopey. Which do you prefer? Violent?" Reuben shook his head. "Guess you want to be dopey? Okay, just make it look good."

I hurried back to Robert and repeated my instruction, adding, "So you're the violent one. When Professor Grimm, or the other man, turn on the machine, you have to wait a minute before you give the Oscar-winning violent performance of your life. Okay?"

Robert nodded.

I slumped onto the floor beside Robert's bed as another more urgent thought raced through my mind. I had overlooked something.

"Listen up, Robert," I whispered. "The machine is unplugged. I've rigged it to look like it's still plugged in. That means no whirring sound or green 'on' light. You will have to perform really well to confuse those men. Your brains will thank you later."

I scrambled over to Reuben to warn him, too. In my excitement, I banged my knee against the metal bed-frame.

"Youch!" I clutched my knee.

Reuben's eyes widened with fear.

Two sets of footsteps again charged into the room.

Grimm and Ihaka stared at me in disbelief.

I stared back at them.

"YOU!" I began, staring at Ihaka, but he showed no recognition of me. "You slimy, two-timing whatever you are—thing."

"Fish. Grimm. See, I s-told you I s-could smell it," bellowed Ihaka. "How did you get in here, girlie? Oh, s-never s-mind. Grab her, Grimm."

Before I could say another word, Grimm grabbed me by the shoulders and clamped his hand over my mouth.

"What's wrong with her face, Grimm? What's that green s-muck on your face, girlie?" said Ihaka, poking his face close to mine. I could smell his foul breath.

"More important, who is she?" replied Grimm. "Who are you?" he said to me.

Grimm eased his hand away from my mouth, just enough for me to answer. I was glad my face camouflage prevented him from recognizing me as the wild cyclist who had ploughed into him.

"Detective Jones is my father," I managed to spit out before he clamped my mouth shut again.

For an instant Ihaka looked stunned; then his lips stretched into a snarl.

"Detective Jones? I remember you s-now. What did I s-tell you about the s-curious pussy s-cat, little girl? What? It s-kills the s-cat, that's what I said—only you didn't listen, did you?"

When I tried to break free from Professor Grimm, he tightened his hold.

"Detective? Did she say her father's a detective, Harry—?" said Grimm, a tremor in his voice.

"So what if he is? Her father is a s-moron. You got nothing to worry about, Grimm. The detective is otherwise occupied. I've seen s-to that."

I stared, unblinking, at Ihaka and aimed a swift kick at his shin.

Missed by a fraction!

"A s-kicking filly, too," he said. "I'll teach you …"

"Wha … what do we do with her?" interrupted Grimm. He was breathing hard and his hands shook.

"s-Package her up like those two," said Ihaka.

"Anyone knows you're here?" asked Grimm.

"Nuffufnm," I mumbled, struggling to break free again.

"What?" he said.

Was Grimm expecting me to answer, with his large hand clamped over my mouth?

I bit down on the fleshy part of his palm, near his little finger. He whipped his hand away from my mouth, but still held me prisoner with his other arm.

"My father does. He will get you two jerks for this."

"She's lying. Here, gag her." Ihaka ripped a piece of packaging tape off the roll.

"How could you, Mr. Ihaka? How could you lie to my father? And what have you done with Frank?"

Harry Ihaka curled his top lip. "This should shut you up, s-kid." He waved the packaging tape in my face.

Professor Grimm tightened his hold on me, while Harry Ihaka slapped the packaging tape across my mouth. I let fly with my right foot and made a solid connection this time with Ihaka's kneecap. He staggered backwards.

"You stupid s-kicking horse …" He raised his hand.

"Stop it, Harry," said Grimm, yanking me sideways as Ihaka's hand crashed down, missing my ear by a hair.

"Know what happens when you stick your s-nose where it doesn't belong, little girl? You end up like that s-nosy s-pussy I've been warning you about."

Ihaka had a mean look in his eyes.

"You want to s-know about that dopey security guard, Frank?" he said. "He's dead. Deader than a s-toenail in over-tight shoes … and you will be, too … soon."

You two-faced rat, I wanted to spit out. But I couldn't because of the tape across my mouth. How I wanted to wipe the smug look off his face.

"Look, Harry, we didn't plan on detective Jones busting in on us," said Grimm. "You said he was staking out Marvel."

"I said don't worry about him." Ihaka grinned. "The s-kid's bluffing. Last time I checked, the s-camper was parked exactly where it has been since Friday—across from s-Marvel's place. Jones was in it. He's not as smart as he s-thinks, and s-neither is his foolish daughter."

"Well, how did she find out about us?" said Grimm. "She's just a kid … yet she ended up here."

"Just s-nosy—like those two," Ihaka jerked his chin towards the twins, "but we'll deal with her later. s-Come, let's get on with the experiment. Fetch the equipment. If it works, we'll scramble her brains too."

They quickly bound my ankles. Now the twins and I were in a right pickle.

At the door, Grimm turned and stared at me. His eyes had softened. Was he beginning to regret his involvement with Ihaka and this whole, nasty business?

I looked at the twins and shrugged my shoulders, all the while praying for a miracle.

Twenty-Four
Guinea-pigs

Minutes later, Grimm returned, carrying a gadget, which looked like an external modem for a computer.

"Hurry, s-man, hurry," said Ihaka. "We don't have all s-night. Besides, they're waiting for s-news of our progress."

"Who's they?" replied Grimm, setting the gadget down beside the SIP.

"s-Never s-mind that right s-now."

"Blast!" said Grimm, looking around. "I thought I'd left a spare extension cord here earlier."

He rushed out of the room, returning within seconds with a long white one. He hooked up the gadget to one end; then plugged the other into a wall outlet.

From his coat pocket, he whipped out a short cable—like the one I had seen on the back seat of Harry Ihaka's car when he first came to see my father. He fastened one end of the cable to the gadget and the other end to the SIP.

He switched on the SIP and the gadget. When nothing happened, he looked behind the SIP. I heard him gasp. He looked at me.

My eyes begged him not to expose what I had done. His eyes glazed over for a moment and his expression softened.

"Let's get on with it." Ihaka stamped his foot.

"No power supply," replied Grimm. His voice seemed different, gentler.

When he looked at me again, there was a faint smile at the corners of his mouth.

"Ah, I see the problem," he said. "Flick the switch on the wall over there, Harry."

The gadget purred to life, then. A tiny green light flickered, but no lights lit up on the SIP.

I held my breath; Robert looked at me.

"Hey, wait a minute," said Grimm. "How come the SIP doesn't look like it's working?"

My hopes sank. I had misjudged Professor Grimm's body language. He was going to reveal my sabotage, after all.

"Don't be stupid s-man. Of s-course it's working," said Ihaka. "It's plugged in, isn't it? And the switch is on, isn't it?"

Again, Grimm checked behind the SIP.

I held my breath.

"Yep, it's plugged in, all right," he said.

I exhaled.

"Then it works. It's not supposed to s-make any s-noise. None of our equipment does, where I s-come from."

The two men stared at the SIP then at the twins.

"Ummm, anytime s-now something interesting should happen," said Ihaka, rubbing his hands together.

I looked at Robert and nodded my head ever so slightly.

Robert took the hint and began to twitch and move his head from side to side. Then he rolled his eyes so only the whites showed. He began to shake as if he were holding on to a drilling machine. He lifted his bound legs, then bounced them repeatedly on the bed.

"We've got action, Grimm. Look, he's acting like a rabid dog. He s-can't s-control his actions. The SIP works, it works."

"But I thought you said it was the other one who is supposed to exhibit violent behavior," said Grimm.

I sucked in my breath, again.

"So I was wrong," Ihaka replied. "What does it s-matter? The experiment is a success—one is violent, while the other remains placid. It is as it should be."

"Good. Then we must stop this now," said Grimm.

"s-No! Increase the intensity," shouted Ihaka.

"Why? Haven't you seen enough?" said Grimm.

"Do it. I want to s-make s-triple sure it works," said Ihaka, his face close to Robert's now.

"As you wish … switching to intensity level 8," said Grimm, bending over the SIP and fiddling with a dial.

On cue, Robert turned up his performance several notches. He began to twitch and vibrate his body with more vigor. When he began snorting like an enraged bull, I began to wonder if the SIP had somehow really begun to work.

"Perfect!" Ihaka rocked back on his heels and clasped his hands behind his back, a triumphant expression on his fat face. "Perfect!"

"I still don't understand it, Harry. Why would the SIP switch itself?"

I held my breath. *Don't do this, Professor,* my eyes pleaded.

"Look it, Grimm, if you feel that strongly about it, let's hook up the girl—see how she reacts," replied Ihaka, walking towards me.

"Oh, all right." Grimm switched off the machines, removed the electrodes from Robert's head, and rolled him to one side.

Harry Ihaka dragged me over to the bed. I offered only token resistance. Grimm attached the electrodes to my forehead. He winked at me, and again a faint smile played at the corners of his mouth.

He switched the machines on again.

"Ummm, give her a blast at fifty s-pulses a s-minute first," said Ihaka, poking his index finger into his ear and jiggling it.

"Fifty? Why not twenty?" said Grimm.

"Make it eighty, then," grunted Ihaka.

Grimm grazed his knuckles against my cheek.

"Intensity set at eighty pulses," he said.

The pleading look on my face and the pained groan was only for effect. Eighty-pulses! I would have to better Robert's performance.

"Good. Anytime s-now you should dance like flames in a fire, kicking filly," said Ihaka bending over me. "I'm going to enjoy the show."

I closed my eyes as a shower of spit rained on my face. With my eyes still closed, I twitched my eyelids; then rolled my eyeballs around. I twitched my nose as if trying to scratch a tickle. I puffed out my cheeks like a blowfish and tried to make buzzing noises against the packaging tape across my mouth. I began to twitch my arms, legs, and torso. I was shaking so hard, my bound wrists shot up, smacking the side of Ihaka's flabby face, hard.

The unexpected impact made him gasp.

"See that?" he said, rubbing his face. "This is as it should be. You have s-not erred in s-programming the s-machine, Grimm. Umm, it works perfectly, like a well oiled s-cow."

"Wheel!" said Grimm. "I've seen enough. What are we going to do with two violent children?"

"Who s-cares, Grimm?" said Ihaka.

"I'm turning off the machines."

"No, wait, Grimm, I'm enjoying this. The famous detective s-Jones's nosy daughter is caught like a fly in a s-trap."

Rat in a trap, you silly alien goat, I yelled inwardly, willing him to bring his face closer again so I could deliver another stinging blow.

Harry Ihaka rubbed his sweaty ham-like hands together, and for effect, I intensified my violent reaction.

"Umm, s-pump it up to ninety s-pulses, Grimm—no, s-make that one hundred."

"That's too high, Harry. You don't want to fry her brains, do you?"

"Do it! I don't give a rat's tailpipe about her brain."

"Behind—rat's behind," said Grimm.

"Whatever ... just get on with it."

"As you wish," muttered Grimm.

This time, when Ihaka brought his face close to mine for a better look, I jerked my body upwards. My bound hands swung up like a pendulum and aimed a stinging blow directly across the bridge of his fat nose.

Ihaka's eyes watered, his nose flared and turned beet red.

"You stupid little—" began Ihaka.

A wood-splintering smash coming from upstairs made him freeze in mid-sentence.

Twenty-Five
My Life or Death
Performance

"What was that?" said Grimm, looking startled.

He and Harry Ihaka stared at each other in disbelief when several sets of footsteps thundered across the kitchen floor, above us.

"Dim the lights, Harry, quick!"

"Grimm?" called out Dr. Marvel's voice. "Where the dickens are you?"

I groaned as loudly as I could, but with the packaging tape plastered across my mouth, I didn't know if the sound would travel as far as the kitchen.

Harry Ihaka charged at me. The back of his hand whacked the side of my face. My eyes watered.

"You hush up, you hear," he said in a hoarse whisper. "Stop the s-machines, Grimm." He motioned with his hand.

Mr. Ihaka trembled and I could see he was struggling to control himself. His eyes bulged. Professor Grimm, looking pale, did not move.

I continued my violent performance. Before Ihaka or Grimm could recover their composure, it was too late—footsteps were already galloping down the stairs.

Everything happened fast. I revved up my violent behavior, jerking and flinging my bound legs against the wall. Ihaka rushed towards the door, but Reuben twisted his body on the bed and flung his legs out. Ihaka tripped and went flying face first to the floor, just as Dr. Marvel burst into the room. Looking like a surprised, yet indignant stork, he hopped over Ihaka, to avoid stepping on him.

"Blinking traffic lights! Booby traps!" said Dr. Marvel, one foot hovering, arms stretched out on either side.

Behind Dr. Marvel, I was surprised to see Bernie and Chico—alias Boraz and Arkon—still wearing their security guards uniform.

"Booby traps everywhere, fellas," repeated Dr. Marvel over his shoulder. "Tread with care. I just stumbled over one. Nearly broke my neck."

He looked down at the squirming Ihaka.

"Grimm, is that you?" he said, lowering his foot. "Trying to squirm your way out, are you? Why is it so dim in here?"

Just then, Boraz reached down and grabbed Ihaka, who was struggling to regain his feet.

In the dim light, I saw Dr. Marvel's hand search the wall beside the open doorway for the light control. With a twist of the control knob, the overhead light brightened.

Dr. Marvel peered at the struggling man on the ground.

"Whoa! You're not Grimm. Declare your identity!" he demanded

"This is Harry Ihaka, the supposed head of security at Te Papa," volunteered Boraz. "And that over there is the missing SIP, or S1M1 unit, as we call it."

Dr. Marvel's eyes locked onto the SIP like lasers. He hadn't noticed the twins or me.

"No one touches the SIP except me," he said, in a commanding voice. But when he stepped towards it, Arkon hooked his foot around his ankle, almost tripping him.

"Oh no you don't, Marvel," said Arkon, pushing Dr. Marvel aside.

Ah ha! I thought, *so Dr. M's one of them all right. I should have guessed. Why else would he rush like that for the SIP?*

But whose side was he on?

"Stop it, both of you," yelled Boraz. He stared at Dr. Marvel and in a commanding voice said, "Return!"

I saw a faint blue light shoot out of Dr. Marvel's left ear and swoop into Boraz's right one.

Dr. Marvel staggered. He jiggled his ear.

"Flaming asteroids, ever since our encounter at Te Papa, I thought something was clogging my receptors and meddling with my thalamus and hypothalamus," he said.

With everyone's attention on the SIP, no one but me heard yet another set of footsteps rushing across the kitchen floor, then down the stairs.

My eyes almost popped out when I saw Dad charging into the room, his face glistening with sweat.

"Ah Marvel, I knew you were up to no good," said Dad stepping over Bernie and Ihaka. "Harry, what's going on? Did Marvel attack you? Are you all right?"

"You're supposed to be the hot-shot s-Canadian detective, so you tell s-me," snarled Ihaka. "Why don't you arrest these baboons?"

Dad looked baffled. When he caught sight of me, his eyes narrowed. At first, he couldn't tell it was me, lying trussed up on the bed, dressed in my black detective gear and green face camouflage. I must have looked a sight, because my father's jaw dropped open and he sucked in his breath.

"Michelle? Is that you? What have they done to your face? What's going on here?" He stood frozen, beads of sweat formed across his top lip.

I made one last realistic display of violent behavior, while keeping my eyes on Professor Grimm.

Dad rushed over and dropped to his knees beside me. His hands hovered over my face. I could tell he didn't want to touch it; he couldn't be sure what the green stuff was.

"God knows I tried to keep you out of trouble, Michelle," he said. "I warned you, but no, you had to get mixed up with Marvel."

Dad reached for the electrodes attached to my forehead, but hesitated to pull them free. He swore under his breath.

"Get these off her, now," he shouted. "If she's hurt, you'll all pay!"

Ihaka broke into a raucous laugh. "s-Too late, detective Jones, she's a goner all right. And s-to think you, of all s-people, s-couldn't recognize when you'd been s-conned. Your daughter's brain is fried crisp, like bacon … there's nothing you s-can do about it. s-Nothing," said Ihaka, trying to break free of the clutches of Bernie and Chico. "s-*Nothing!*" he repeated, his face twisting into ugliness. He burst out laughing again.

"He who laughs last … laughs last," said Dr. Marvel, stabbing the air with his right index finger.

"For Pete's sake, man, turn off the equipment," Dad snapped over his shoulder at Grimm.

He reached out and ripped the packaging tape off my mouth, taking with it some of my green facemask. Then he began ripping through the tape that bound my wrists.

Dad's hands were shaking; sweat dripped off his chin. I could have reassured him that I was all right, but I wanted to fool Ihaka a little longer.

"Marvel, you're going to be sorry you got my daughter into this mess," said Dad. His breathing was raspy.

Harry Ihaka jerked his chin towards me, his face full of malice.

"Too late, Jones, her brain's useless now," he said. "But you sure s-could use her to scare off s-possums. Just look at her. She s-can't s-control herself."

"What does that mean, Harry? What do you know about this?" Dad demanded.

"Look for yourself, detective. She's fried."

Poor Dad. He had no idea what was going on.

I decided to stop my performance.

"Harry Ihaka, or whoever you are, you don't know how dumb you sound. Maybe it's *your* brain that was indirectly altered," I blurted, jerking myself to a sitting position. The electrodes peeled away from my forehead.

"Eh?" said Ihaka. He looked stunned.

"The SIP was never powered up because I unplugged it earlier," I said.

"SIP?" Dad's eyes bulged in disbelief. He fumbled with the last of the packaging tape that bound my ankles.

Pushing myself off the bed, I reached behind the SIP and lifted the cables to reveal how I had tampered with them.

"Bravo! Caveat emptor!" said Dr. Marvel, when my father remained speechless. "Now what else do you have to babble about that, Ihaka? The child has outwitted you."

"S-meddling little s-pest, more like," shouted Mr. Ihaka in disbelief. "S-confound her! What s-kind of an expert are you, Grimm?"

"Ah, Grimm," said Dr. Marvel, "I knew you were up to no good when that package was delivered to my house tonight in error. Moa Lane and Moa Road—anyone could have got them mixed up. After the fellow left, I put my gray matter to work. Those kids were on to something. Bernie and Chico arrived at my abode just as I was mobilizing for action—a shoot-out at Grimm's corral."

"Will someone explain what's going on?" said my dad, looking bewildered.

It was the first time I had seen such a lost expression on his face. Dad was always first at unraveling a mystery, but not this time.

"Well, my boy," said Dr. Marvel, rocking back on his heels, his hands thrust deep inside his coat pockets. He assumed his characteristic kidney-bean posture. "You have no idea, do you? Imagine spying on me all this time, when you should have been spying on Grimm and Ihaka."

"How did you know it was me in the camper-van?" said my father, one eyebrow arched.

"I'm a scientist, Sonny. I have my methods. I knew the Buchanan's were planning a holiday, but I didn't believe they would hire a camper-van just to holiday in their own driveway. What I couldn't figure out was why you were spying on me." He squinted at Dad. "So, why *were* you spying on me, eh?"

Dad sighed. A vein pulsed madly at his temple.

"You must have been watching my every move, to have followed me here tonight," continued Dr. Marvel.

Dad scratched his jaw. "Yes, I was watching you from the start. I had good reason to believe you had stolen the SIP. I was waiting for you to slip up. You sure were acting strange these past few days. Then, when the deliveryman showed up at your house tonight, I thought I had you. Who makes deliveries on a Sunday evening? But when you had two more visitors, I knew something was going to happen. When the three of you charged out of your front door like pit bulls, I had to follow. I was sure my painstaking surveillance was about to pay dividends."

"Moi?" replied Dr. Marvel. "You thought I had uplifted the SIP? For what purpose? Someone was prepared to go to a lot of trouble to discredit me if they paid you to sit on your hind quarters, just to see if I was a common thief."

"Are you saying I was misled on purpose, Marvel?" Dad squared his shoulders.

"I would jolly well say so. Do I look like a criminal, detective?"

"Everyone knows how eccentric you are, Marvel, forever inventing some nonsense. So, why wouldn't you get involved in something as crazy as this? It's the kind of thing you'd do for attention, isn't it?" Dad's face was beet red.

Dr. Marvel stuck his chin out, as though he might poke it in Dad's eye. "I suggest you direct your suspicions to those two." He pointed with his index finger to Harry Ihaka and Professor Grimm.

"Them? Marvel you're a lunatic," said Dad. "For your information, Harry Ihaka is the head of security. It was he who arranged for the camper-van to be placed ..." Dad's voice trailed off.

Dr. Marvel shook his head and shrugged in despair.

"Bind Ihaka's wrists, fellas," he said to Bernie and Chico, who now had their knees on Mr. Ihaka's back, pinning him to the floor. "Prop him up against the bed." He turned to glower at Professor Grimm who was cowering in the corner, still holding the extension cable. "And you, what ...?"

"I wasn't a willing accomplice in this mess, honest," stammered Professor Grimm.

"Likely story," said Dr. Marvel.

Reuben groaned. That's when Dad and Dr. Marvel focused on the twins for the first time.

"Geez!" Dad exclaimed, scrambling over to Reuben and peeling the packaging tape and electrodes off him. Reuben shifted to a sitting position, rubbing his mouth.

"So, you kids were about to become stir-fried vegetables," said Dr. Marvel rescuing Robert.

"Dr. M, is that you in there?" I asked, for I had never seen him act so controlled.

"Of course it's me, Millie-girl. What makes you ask?"

"Just wanted to make sure, that's all." I squeezed his hand, before turning my attention to the Professor.

"What's your part in all of this?" I asked. It was you who left a message on my dad's answering machine, wasn't it? It was you, in disguise, that he met the other night on Moa Lane, wasn't it? You led him to believe Dr. Marvel was the one who stole the SIP, didn't you? You even wanted money for the false information. You set up my dad."

Dad sucked in his breath, obviously shocked at my accusation.

Professor Grimm's eyes darted from my father to the men holding Harry Ihaka on the floor.

"Look, I had no idea, honest," he said. "Ihaka persuaded me to do this thing. He convinced me it was important research work for our prison population."

"A likely story," said Dad, recovering his composure.

"That's what they all say," chimed in Dr. Marvel.

Grimm rubbed his chin.

Suddenly, I felt sorry for him. Perhaps he was telling the truth.

"When I realized what I was about to do to the twins, I wanted to sabotage the operation, but I just didn't seem to have the will-power, until I saw your daughter had already—" he began.

Just then, Ihaka wriggled and grunted like a wild animal trapped against its will. My heart pumped as I watched him struggle with Boraz and Arkon who had not yet bound his wrists. Exerting all his might, Harry Ihaka managed to wrench himself free. He scrambled to his feet and rushed towards the SIP. Just as he was about to grab it, Boraz dove at his knees in a flying tackle. Ihaka fell backwards on top of him; Arkon jumped on top of Ihaka. The three of them made a peculiar-looking sandwich.

Twenty-Six
Saja Revealed

"What's going on?" said Dad, staring at the piled up bodies.

"Help me, please … somebody," said Harry Ihaka in a low voice.

To me, it sounded like the real Mr. Ihaka's desperate cry for help. No one else seemed to have heard, though.

"Look, detective Jones," gasped a breathless Boraz, from the bottom of the pile, "this man isn't really Harry Ihaka."

"What is that supposed to mean?" said Dad. "He's your boss, isn't he?"

"Not really," said Arkon.

"You two are the Te Papa security guards I saw earlier today." Dad was short on patience. "Then this must be your boss."

"Look, we can make him tell you who he really is," said Boraz. "Just get him off me, Arkon, will you?"

"Just who are you?" said Dad.

"Not security guards, that's for sure," said Boraz, once Arkon rolled Harry Ihaka off him.

With Dad and Dr. Marvel's help, they bound Ihaka's wrists and ankles with packaging tape and left him sitting on the floor, propped against the front of the desk. His head drooped between his hunched shoulders. He made more grunting sounds and his body convulsed.

Arkon produced a flat yellow disc, the size of a five-cent coin, from his pocket and planted it in the center of Ihaka's forehead. The disc seemed to attach itself to the skin. Ihaka stopped wriggling and his head jerked upright.

"This will isolate Saja's thoughts and allow us to access his plans," said Arkon. "It will act like a truth serum, but won't dull his senses."

He nodded to Boraz. "Go ahead."

"Who are you?" said Boraz.

"I am Saja, leader of the rebel army on planet Zorb," said Harry Ihaka's voice. "Who are you?"

"We ask the questions," said Boraz. "Why are you here?"

"To take possession of the SIP, the machine my enemies, Arkon and Boraz, invented. It holds the minds of their people—the ones I have already captured."

"How did you uplift the SIP from Te Papa?" said Boraz.

"That was easy. I used Grimm to do it."

"How?"

"I controlled his mind for a time."

"What did you do to the SIP?" continued Boraz.

"I had Grimm alter it for my purposes."

"What did he do exactly?"

"Under my direction, he has programmed it to scramble minds. I made him dispose of the paperwork."

"Arkon and Boraz can stop you from taking the machine," said Boraz, knowing that Saja could not recognize him in his human body.

"Never!" said Saja. "They must be dead by now. Otherwise they would have been more vigilant in protecting the machine. They were stupid enough to think they could hide it in a storehouse on Earth."

Saja laughed.

"Fools!" he continued. "No one outsmarts me. I had little trouble tracking down the SIP. All I needed was a human body, a stooge, and a diversion to complete my plan."

Saja glared at the rest of us. His nose twitched.

"Fish! It stinks in here," he said, rubbing his right shoulder against his nose.

"Why do you keep smelling fish when no one else can?" I asked, marveling at the fluency of Saja's speech, now that he was under the influence of the disc.

"That's how you Earth people smell to me, like stinking, rotting fish. Bah!"

I glared at Saja. "You're ugly and mean."

Saja, in Ihaka's body, bared his teeth at me then turned to Boraz.

"With Arkon and Boraz dead, my control of their people is inevitable," he said. "It's only a matter of time before I escape this stinking planet of yours. No one can stop me now."

"Is that enough for you, detective Jones?" said Boraz.

My father could only nod.

Boraz removed the disc from Ihaka's forehead, and immediately his head slumped onto his chest once more. Saja was silent, as if he were asleep.

Dad looked stunned. He cleared his throat. "If you two are not really Te Papa security guards, you must be—"

"Alien scientists from planet Zorb," I said.

"Zorb? The tenth planet?" said Dad, one eyebrow raised.

I nodded. "Zat is correct, doubting Earthling."

"And you and Dr. Marvel already knew this?" Disbelief flooded his eyes.

"Affirmative, Dad, but it's a long story."

"I want to know now, Michelle!"

"Later, Dad, it's a long story."

Dad took a long, deep breath then released it, one puff at a time. He cracked his knuckles.

"And the twins? How did they get tangled up in this mess? What do they know?" he asked.

"At the moment not a lot, because of those secrecy bands on their wrists," I replied.

"Secrecy what?" Dad flopped down on the bed beside Robert, grabbed his wrist, and examined the band. "Where'd you get it?"

The twins looked at each other.

"From Dr. M," I answered when Robert didn't. "They were supposed to keep the boys out of trouble."

Dad turned to Dr. Marvel. "Explain."

Dr. Marvel scratched his head. "A trap, no doubt, had been set to ensnare the lads. What bait did you use, Grimm?"

"How dare you!" said Professor Grimm "Look, it was Ihaka who caught them snooping and—"

Something heavy crashed onto the main floor, directly above our heads.

Dad jumped up. "What was that?"

"They're holding someone hostage in one of the rooms upstairs," I said.

Dad and Boraz scrambled up the stairs. Arkon remained to keep guard over Harry Ihaka, while Dr. Marvel pinned Professor Grimm with a warning stare.

The twins and I just waited.

I could hear muffled voices. Above us, floorboards creaked and groaned as footsteps tramped across the wood floor and thundered down the stairs to where we were.

Twenty-Seven
Professor Grimm Confesses

Dad and Boraz stumbled into the room, awkwardly supporting another man between them. He was wearing a Te Papa security guard's uniform. He was disheveled, and his face was shadowed by several days' growth.

"Eee-ha! Not another maverick?" said Dr. Marvel, his eyes wide. "Is he from planet Zorb, too?"

Dr. Marvel raced over to the man and pinched his nose.

"Well are you from Zorb?" he asked. "Speak up, man, speak up. You have a mouth-like appendage on your face. Use it ... like this." He demonstrated by clanking his jaws together.

"Get this maniac off me." The newcomer pulled his head away from Dr. Marvel's assault.

"This one belongs to your planet," said Boraz.

"Ha! I knew that—but I had to make sure," said Dr. Marvel, his moustache twitching like a mouse's whiskers.

"This is Frank. He's going to fill in some missing pieces," said Dad.

"Frank!" I exclaimed. "Mr. Ihaka said you were dead."

"Well I ain't no spook, okay?" Frank choked out.

"Another piece of the jigsaw!" said Dr. Marvel, rocking back on his heels. "I'll be darned."

Frank, the security guard, smoothed a crease from his crumpled Te Papa uniform with trembling fingers. He looked dazed.

"What's going on here ... Bernie ... Chico ...?" He stopped in mid-sentence; his gaze locked onto Professor Grimm. "You son of a ..." He lunged unsteadily at the Professor, who tottered back on his heels.

"Easy, fella," said Dad, restraining Frank.

Frank got yet another shock when he saw his boss trussed up like a sack of potatoes.

"Mr. Ihaka, sir," he said. "Why have they strung you up?" He turned towards Dad. "He ain't no crook? He's the head of security at Te Papa. Bernie, Chico, didn't you tell 'em?"

"Ah!" said Dr. Marvel. "What the eyes at first behold must always be questioned. You may perceive the person you see to be Ihaka, because the shell he wears for a body appears thus. Likewise, you may think the same of Bernie and Chico … but I can assure you, son, your eyes deceive you."

"And who are *you*? Einstein or Sherlock Holmes?" Frank gaped at Dr. Marvel.

"Huuummm … neither! I'm Dr. Marvel, retired scientist—at your service." Dr. Marvel bowed so low, the tip of his nose almost touched his kneecap.

"When you're ready, Frank, just tell us how you came to be locked up in Grimm's bedroom," said Dad, motioning him to sit on the bed, beside Reuben.

"I've done nothin' but sit these last few days," said Frank, "right now all I wanna do is get my hands on *him*." He glared at Professor Grimm. "Even without his get-up, I recognize the scoundrel!"

"What get-up? Start at the beginning, man," said Dr. Marvel, growing impatient.

Frank rubbed the back of his neck and rotated his head a few times.

"Last Thursday I was doing my rounds, just before Te Papa closed for the evening, you know, making sure the patrons were all moving their butts towards the exit," he paused.

"Then what?" prompted Dr. Marvel.

"I was near the Star Trek display when that man walked up to me. I'd recognize those beady eyes anywhere, even without his ponytail and moustache." He pointed to Professor Grimm.

"Then what happened?" asked Dad.

"He said he was on official business. He didn't look official to me, even though his orange overalls had Department of National Security stamped across the front. He waved a bunch of papers in my face and said they authorized him to collect the SIP. I had no idea what the SIP was, and said so."

Professor Grimm cleared his throat.

"The man looked uncomfortable," continued Frank. "His eyes darted around the displays like he was nervous. Before I could shout for help, he pounced on me like a starving jackal. I felt a sharp jab in my arm.

"When he released me, he was holding a hypodermic needle and he had a smirk on his face. He said I was to follow his instructions. He walked over to one of the displays and removed a piece of equipment, which looked something like a laptop computer. Yeah, that's it, over there!"

Frank pointed to the SIP.

"Go on," encouraged my father.

"Well, whatever was in the hypodermic must have numbed my brain pretty good, because my body felt heavy and my limbs were useless. I couldn't even scream for help when the man pulled out an empty backpack from inside his overalls, and slipped the laptop into it. He slung the backpack over his shoulders.

"He whipped off my cap, removed my baton, and dropped them on the floor. He said it had to look as if I had either stumbled on a robbery or assisted in one, except I wasn't going to be around to explain."

Frank paused, but kept his eyes locked on Professor Grimm.

"Then what happened?" prompted Dr. Marvel.

"The next thing I knew, I was staggering out of the Star Trek exhibit. No one else was on the floor now. The man all but carried me towards the rear exit." Frank paused again.

"Come on man ... get on with it," insisted Dr. Marvel.

Frank took a quick breath. "He forced me into a minivan. We left Te Papa unnoticed. When we got to Molesworth Street, the man pulled over near the Deloitte building. He jabbed me with another needle and I passed out.

"When I woke up, I was bound and gagged and sitting on the floor up there." He jerked his chin towards the ceiling. "And that's where I've been for the past few days ... no shower, nothing."

"No food either?" I asked.

"He fed me, all right, but only after I promised not to yell. I sure could use a shower," said Frank, with a sniff.

"If it weren't for the fact you were incarcerated in Grimm's abode, I would dismiss your tale as pure fiction, akin to Planet of the Apes," said Dr. Marvel, rocking on his heels. "What are your deductions, Mr. Detective?"

Dad drew in a deep breath and exhaled it through pursed lips.

"Assault ... kidnapping ... theft ... aliens! Sounds like something out of Hollywood." He answered, wiping his brow with the back of his hand. "Grimm, how come you got involved in this mess in the first place?"

Professor Grimm shook his head as if to clear it.

"I don't recall exactly," he answered. "Was I involved? It's not possible! A man of my reputation couldn't be entangled in a crime such as this. This is preposterous."

Professor Grimm pulled out a wallet from his back pocket.

"Look here, detective, this is who I am—a citizen of high moral values and integrity, worthy of the OBE—Order of the British Empire, should her Majesty the Queen of England see fit."

He held out the wallet so Dad could see his ID.

"I wouldn't trust him, Dad. It's just propaganda," I said, instantly regretting my comment.

Dr. Marvel groaned. "Sounds more like proper-goose if you ask me."

"It is obvious that he's still under Saja's influence," interrupted Boraz, coming forward with the disc he had used on Mr. Ihaka. He planted the disc on Professor Grimm's forehead despite his weak protests.

"Bernie," said Frank, "What are you doing?"

"He's harnessing the mind that is the man," said Dr. Marvel. "But Bernie is not quite who you think he is, at this point in the space-time tablecloth."

Frank looked confused and exasperated. He clamped his hands on his hips and widened his stance.

"If he's not Bernie, then how come he looks so much like him?" he demanded. "Here, what's really going on?"

"Sssssh!" said Dr. Marvel. "Observe."

The rest of us knew what to expect and we waited with baited breath for Boraz to begin his interrogation.

"Now Professor," he said. "Who are you?"

"I'm Gregory Roland Ignacious Milton Mistletoe. You will note that my initials spell my surname. I am a retired professor, now self-employed as an information technology consultant. I am also a part-time paleontologist."

Professor Grimm stuck his chest out and pulled his shoulders back.

Dad cleared his throat.

Dr. Marvel tried to suppress a smile.

I was thinking, Professor G-R-I-M-M Grimm.

Suddenly, Grimm's body went into convulsions.

"What's happening to him?" I asked.

"The part of Saja that's in him is trying to resist the power of the disc," replied Arkon.

"How did you become involved with Saja, Professor?" asked Boraz.

Grimm coughed, his convulsing abated.

"It was remarkable really," he said slowly. "After my customary six kilometer jog last Thursday evening, I was watching the Holmes show as I was having my tea. All of a sudden, the TV screen glowed red and the picture became distorted.

"Thinking something was wrong, I got up to adjust the aerial. A voice coming from the TV told me to freeze. I froze with my hand outstretched. Then the voice said I was to do what I was told. Then it said I should drive to Te Papa where I would be given further instructions. The voice told me there was a bag beside my chair and I should get it." Grimm sucked in a slow, deep breath.

"Get on with it, man," said Dr. Marvel.

"Huh! Yes, well ..." began Grimm. "I felt compelled to do as I was told. To my surprise, I found a bag, just as he had said. Inside the bag were a wig, a bushy moustache, and a pair of orange overalls. I was told to put them on. Like a robot, I again did as I was told. I was then instructed to drive to Te Papa." Professor Grimm paused.

"What happened after you uplifted the SIP?" said Boraz.

"The voice told me I had to take the security guard hostage because we couldn't risk exposure, just yet. It also told me to mention the name Harry Ihaka, if I should have any problems."

Again, Grimm lapsed into silence.

"What happened after you arrived home?" Dad prompted.

"I half-carried him into the house, bound and gagged him with tape, and left him on the bedroom floor. Poor fellow, he was out for hours. Then Harry Ihaka showed up with instructions for me to reprogram the machine. He had all the details in his head and I had to write them down on a sheet of paper. I was to eat the paper after I'd completed the reprogramming."

"And did you, Professor?" said Boraz.

"Did I what?"

"Eat the paper."

"What paper?"

"The one with the reprogramming instructions," said Boraz, tapping Grimm's forehead. "Remember?"

"Ah! Good heavens no. Well, yes. I ate some of it, but it tasted like crap. I don't eat crap, do you?"

"Crap?" said Boraz, tilting his head to one side.

"Heard of toilet?" I asked.

Surely, somewhere in the real Bernie's brain, there must be a definition of that word.

"That's enough, Michelle," said Dad, clearing his throat. "So where is the rest of the paper, then?"

"Right here."

Grimm removed one shoe and lifted the inside sole. He pulled out a folded piece of notepaper.

"Hope it's not too sweaty," he said.

A cheesy smell permeated the air.

"Thanks, I'll take that," said Arkon and jammed the paper into his pocket. "We'll need it to reverse what you have done."

"Were you aware of the purpose of the machine, Professor?" said Boraz.

"No, not until tonight, when Harry told me about it. He said it could be useful to control prisoners."

"He lied." Boraz removed the disc from Professor Grimm's forehead.

"Well, Frank, is this the Bernie you know?" asked Dr. Marvel. "I think not."

"Hadn't we better get the cops here?" said Frank. "I don't know about the rest of you, but something doesn't add up."

"No!" said Dad. "No cops. This is not an Earth problem, Frank. This has to be sorted here and now. What I'd like to know is why Harry Ihaka contacted me with some trumped-up story about the SIP being stolen? Why, Harry?"

"It's no use asking him, pal," said Dr. Marvel. "He's not going to tell unless they jab that disc thing back on his noggin, right between his bushy eyebrows. I can't wait to hear what he'll belch out this time."

"Me too," I said.

Boraz slapped the disc back on Harry Ihaka's forehead. He moaned; then opened his eyes.

"Who are you?" said Boraz.

"Saja, you idiot … I told you so before. What do you got for brains? A sieve?"

"Why did you retain detective Jones?" Boraz asked.

Saja laughed a harsh resounding laugh. "To keep him occupied. I had him eating out of my hand."

"Why?" asked Boraz.

"I had to make the nincompoop believe the theft of the SIP was highly confidential and that no one except him and me should know about it. He believed every word I said. I needed to create a diversion—just for a few days. I made Grimm arrange a phony late-night meeting with Jones to tell him that Marvel was a prime suspect." Saja licked his parched lips.

Dad cracked his knuckles.

Dr. Marvel sucked in his breath, but said nothing.

"Continue, Saja," said Boraz.

Saja cleared his throat. "Then, I made Ihaka rent a camper-van for Jones to stake out the suspect. When I saw him in it, I knew I had succeeded in setting him to chase after the wrong rabbit. I didn't count on his nosy daughter interfering. I should have drained her brain that day when I told her what happens to snooping pussy cats."

"Why you fat, roly-poly can't-walk-in-a-pair-of-shoes, silly goat!" I balled my hands into tight fists, and jumped up, ready to let fly.

"No, Fifi, don't," said Dad, knowing I was likely to follow through with my threat. "After all, it's not the real Harry Ihaka's who's talking."

"Is there any way I can get hold of that rat Saja, then?" My eyes blazed.

"That's what I'd like to know too," said Dad in low tones.

"Yes, Boraz, how do we separate Saja from Harry? And when do you return control of those bodies to the real owners?" asked Dr. Marvel.

"Let's just deal with Saja first," replied Arkon.

I saw fire in Boraz's eyes and beads of sweat forming across his forehead.

"Prepare for separation, Arkon," he whispered. "We must do it."

"It's not going to be easy," Arkon whispered back. "Saja is too clever to allow it. He has occupied that body too long. If we're not careful we might separate Harry Ihaka from his own body, instead of Saja."

"Don't you think I know that?" replied Boraz. "We'll have to take our chances."

"What's holding you, fellas?" asked Dr. Marvel of Boraz and Arkon. "Can't you just command the scoundrel to come forth?"

Twenty-Eight
Saja Captured

"Come forth?" Saja burst into harsh laughter again. "You're *all* fools, especially this crackpot. Command? I cannot be commanded!"

He drew a deep breath.

"All this time wasted on sorting out exactly what's happened has only allowed me to grow stronger, more resistant to what you two jokers can come up with." He jutted his chin towards Arkon and Boraz.

"As it is right now, I can slip into and out of this pathetic body at will," he continued. "Trouble is you can't tell the difference, can you, dummies?"

Saja yanked the disc from his forehead.

"Like I said, idiots," he mocked, "you s-can't s-tell, s-can you? Well, good-bye, I'm about to leave this borrowed frame—or s-maybe I won't. s-Maybe I'll s-take it with s-me to Zorb. Ihaka will be s-no s-more than a specimen for my people. They've never seen a blob before. Goodbye, fools! Stand back and enjoy this moment of s-my victory."

Saja threw his head back and laughed.

"Boraz, do something? Don't let him get away," I whispered. "Can't you use the disc to delete him? It's obviously him when he keeps adding an 's' to his words."

"No, Michelle, it's not that simple. Just as Saja can't identify us while we're occupying human bodies, we can't be certain when he's in total control of Ihaka's body. We can't count on his speech pattern either. I can use a tranquil-izer dart to neutralize him, if we are certain it's really Saja in control, but if we're wrong, it could destroy Harry Ihaka's mind. We can't risk that."

"You got that right," mocked Saja.

It was unbelievable. Saja was threatening to leave, and there was nothing Boraz, or Arkon could do to prevent him. Saja was laughing so hard, it made Harry Ihaka's rotund tummy jiggle.

There had to be a way to entrap Saja, and I had to find it.

Come on Michelle. Think!

"Hang on a minute, Saja … or Mr. Ihaka," I said. "Aren't you forgetting something? You haven't won yet, not without the SIP."

"When I choose to leave, the SIP leaves with s-me. You'll see, little Miss s-curious s-cat."

Harry Ihaka looked at Frank with a surprised, but friendly, smile on his face.

"What are you doing here, mate?" he said. "How's your Mom these days? I often remember the great times she and I had at junior school."

Frank scrambled over to Mr. Ihaka and kneeled beside him.

"Mr. Ihaka? It is you, isn't it?" he said with relief. "Thank God. We thought that horrible Saja had done something dreadful to you. Are you all right, sir?"

Frank seemed convinced, but I still had my doubts.

Harry Ihaka nodded and his lips stretched into a smile, exposing his top row of teeth.

"s-Turkey!"

"That's not Mr. Ihaka," I said.

Saja is clever all right, I thought.

Frank shot me an angry look.

"Of course it's Mr. Ihaka," he yelled. "He and my mother were classmates. Who else would know that?"

"Indeed! Who else? She should have been my wife," Harry Ihaka—or perhaps Saja—answered.

An idea burst into my mind like a spotlight. I knew exactly how to ensnare him.

"Where exactly are you from, Mr. Ihaka?" I said.

"Where exactly am I from? I already told you. s-Papa s-Two s-Toes. Shall I spell it for you?" He closed his eyes and slouched against the desk. His lips stretched into a contented smirk. "P-a-p-a t-w-o—"

I gave Boraz an urgent, meaningful look. In a flash, he placed a small tube between his lips and shot a white, dart-like object towards Harry Ihaka's body. It fastened to his temple.

Saja made feeble attempts to bat the dart away, but his arm flopped to his side like a limp sail.

"Gotcha, Saja the fool." I clapped in triumph.

"Why did you do that?" said Frank, reaching to pull the dart out, but Arkon was there in an instant, pushing Frank's arm aside.

"Sorry, mate, that's not Ihaka," said Arkon. "Saja was still trying to trick us, but we've got him now."

"Thanks, Michelle, Papa Two Toes was the clincher," said Boraz. "Now we'll be able to finish reprogramming the SIP, once we return to Zorb."

I watched in amazement, as the white dart started to turn purple. Mr. Ihaka's body broke into a succession of spasms. His eyes popped wide open and rolled upwards, until only the whites were visible. Sweat poured down his face.

"This is not over," muttered Saja. "You s-can't s-do this."

Saja belched and coughed at the same time. Harry Ihaka's body vibrated so much; I expected his roll-necked sweater and pants to split, like the Hulk. But soon, he became limp and lifeless as a rag doll.

"Good, he's paralyzed now," breathed Boraz. "Activate the SIP, Arkon. Make ready for mind separation."

In the ensuing silence, you could almost count the pounding of heartbeats in the room.

Arkon reached behind the SIP and plugged it in, while Boraz grabbed the suction cups and attached them to Harry Ihaka's temples.

"Wait, you can't take Mr. Ihaka's mind," I piped up.

"No, Michelle. We're only transferring Saja's mind to the SIP. Mr. Ihaka's will remain intact."

The rest of us stayed silent. Boraz punched several keys on the SIP's keyboard. Chimes sounded. He punched two more keys and a row of lights flickered across the keyboard. They continued to blink like Christmas lights. After a few minutes they stopped.

"Got it!" said Arkon with a deep sigh.

Boraz removed the suction cups. Harry Ihaka's body slumped forward, a lock of hair flopping over his eyes.

Dr. Marvel released a long, slow breath.

"Now what happens to him?" said Dr. Marvel, jutting his chin towards Mr. Ihaka.

"He'll soon recover," said Arkon.

"But where's the physical part of Saja?" I asked.

"Still tranquillized in Ihaka's body," replied Arkon. "We'll extract him—but we must be ready to vaporize ourselves, too, so we can escort him back to our planet."

"Eh?" said Dad, his eyes wide in astonishment. "Vaporize?"

"Arkon means we have to be ready to relinquish our borrowed bodies immediately after we effect final separation of Saja from Ihaka's body," said Boraz. "Once that's done, we can safely board our craft and return to Zorb with the SIP and the incapacitated Saja."

"But the SIP isn't properly programmed to restore your peoples' minds, Boraz," I pointed out.

"With Saja captured," said Boraz, "there is little chance of interference from his people once we're back on Zorb. Arkon and I will rectify what Grimm has done and set in motion the program that will restore the minds of our people."

"Now, we must prepare to return these borrowed bodies to their rightful owners," said Arkon. "To tell the truth, I find it quite restricting—having such a heavy body to drag around all day."

"Yes, me too," said Boraz, removing the packaging tape from Harry Ihaka's wrists and ankles.

"What exactly do you look like?" asked Dad.

"You'll see," said Dr. Marvel. "You'll see."

Just then, the real Harry Ihaka regained consciousness. When he realized he was sitting on the floor, he tried to pull himself up.

"Wos goin' on?" he asked.

His mouth moved in a lop-sided fashion, as if he had received numbing injections from the dentist.

"Why c-can't I m-move?" he said with a struggle.

"You're temporarily paralyzed," replied Boraz. "You'll be fine in a few minutes. Please remain calm."

"Bernie … Chico … Frank … why are we … here?" said Harry Ihaka, looking frightened. "And these people … who are they?"

"Mr. Ihaka," began Frank, combing his fingers through his hair. "You won't believe this, but … detective?" he looked at my father.

"I'll explain everything later, Mr. Ihaka," said Dad. "I'm private investigator, Alwyn Jones. Right now, you're about to witness an extraordinary moment as these two, who are not the Bernie and Chico you're familiar with, prepare for their transformation and departure."

"Just try not to freak out … any of you," advised Dr. Marvel.

Boraz walked over to the SIP and punched two keys on the keyboard.

"Ready, Arkon? This is where we say goodbye to these friendly Earth people."

"Ahem," Dr. Marvel cleared his throat. "You don't suppose I could journey back with you, do you?"

Boraz shook his head. "Not this time, Dr. Marvel. Your molecular structure does not make it possible to dematerialize."

"But if you can keep progressing with your interstellar experiments, who knows, one day we might be able to communicate with you directly," said Arkon.

"Will someone *please* ... explain?" said Harry Ihaka, weakly.

"I will, as soon as these men ... er ... beings, leave," said my father.

"What will become of Saja?" I asked.

"As soon as we return to our planet, Boraz and I will develop a program to deactivate Saja and his rebels—once we've rounded them up."

"Deactivate? Like kill them," I said.

"No, Michelle. We don't believe in premature death. Saja and his rebels will have their brains altered."

"Like a lobotomy?" piped up Robert.

"You're going to do brain surgery on them?" said Reuben.

"In a manner of speaking, yes," said Boraz.

"But instead of a surgical incision in the lobe of the brain, we implant a minute chip, like a computer chip, into the cerebellum. This will neutralize all violent thoughts. Saja and his rebels will no longer pursue violence."

"Now there's something that could benefit certain factions of our Earth population," said Dr. Marvel.

"And make my job obsolete?" said Dad.

"Not for some years, gentlemen," said Arkon.

"Thank you for helping us Dr. Marvel and Michelle." said Boraz, bowing slightly. "And Michelle, only nine normal planets will appear on your project. Human scientists have not discovered Zorb, just yet. You have a bright future." He winked and smiled. Then he looked at the puzzled Harry Ihaka. "Come, Saja, it's time to go."

I sat bolt upright, half-expecting to see Saja materialize, like Boraz had in Dr. Marvel's living room—naked and with platypus feet. Instead, a hazy orange vapor began to drift from Mr. Ihaka's body. It hung in the air like wispy angel hair, fanned by a gentle breeze. When the vapor had poured out, Boraz turned once more to us.

"Farewell, my friends." He and Arkon closed their eyes, and for a moment remained motionless, but erect.

I felt sad as I watched blue vapor emanate from the bodies of Bernie and Chico.

"Bye Boraz. Bye Arkon," I said, feeling my eyes sting. "I'll miss you."

"And we ... you," came Boraz's garbled response.

As if in a daze, we watched the SIP vaporize as well. The power cord flopped to the floor. Now the blue vapors surrounded the orange vapor. Then, as if someone had flung a chimney flue wide open, they swooped upwards through the ceiling and disappeared.

Dr. Marvel stood transfixed. He raised his right hand and did a Spock-like splayed-fingers salute.

"Live long and prosper," he said softly.

"So you *are* a Trekkie, aren't you, Dr. M!" I whispered.

He smiled and his eyes twinkled. He picked up the discarded power cord form the SIP.

"Grimm, you don't mind if I kept this, do you?"

Twenty-Nine
Wrapping Up

Bernie and Chico, whose limp bodies had slumped forward after Boraz and Arkon left, tottered to their feet. They would have fallen flat on their faces, had Dad and Frank not caught them.

As if coming out of a trance, Bernie rubbed his eyes.

"Frank? What's with the beard, mate?" he said and looked around. "What's going on? Who are you people? What's happened to the Star Trek exhibits? Where is this place?"

Then his eyes popped wide open.

"Harry? Chico? Why are we all … here?" he asked.

"I'm just as flabbergasted as you," said Mr. Ihaka.

"You two think *you're* confused," said Chico. "Last thing I remember was going to check on you, Frank, at the Star Trek exhibits."

"It sure is a relief to hear you guys talking normal again," said Frank, scratching the three-day growth on his face.

"Well, at least you lot can remember *something*," said Harry Ihaka, relieved to be himself again. "I can't for the life of me recall how I got here …" He pulled a handkerchief from his back pocket and mopped his nose. "… or why my nose should feel as if I've banged it into a wall."

I drew in a deep breath and chewed on my lower lip, feeling sorry for the blow I had let fly on his nose when I did my life and death performance.

Professor Grimm cleared his throat; maybe he remembered, too.

"Well, fellas," said Dr. Marvel to Bernie and Chico. "It's time we explained what happened to you. You might think it a little far-fetched, but I can assure you, it isn't."

"Hang on, Dr. Marvel," said Dad. "Why don't we move to some place more comfortable? This room gives me the heebie-jeebies."

"Yes," said Professor Grimm, "and I would say this calls for something to help us relax. I have just the thing."

Professor Grimm rushed out of the room; we followed. We must have looked a strange sight—seven assorted adults and three kids trooping out of Professor Grimm's basement in the middle of the night!

Dad pulled his cell phone out of his pocket. He punched a few buttons on the keypad. I heard him tell Mom we were fine, though we'd had an extraordinary night.

"Boy, do we have a story to tell you. See you soon, love," he finished.

The twins and I sat together on the floor in the living room. I was anxious to try Professor Grimm's relaxant, whatever that was.

Soon he returned from the kitchen carrying a tray stacked with glasses, a decanter of dry sherry, and a bottle of Ginger Ale.

The Ginger Ale he poured into three large glasses, which he handed to us kids. Then he poured generous portions of sherry into some smaller glasses.

"Don't we kids get any sherry to relax us after the ordeal we went through, Professor?" I asked.

I held out my glass.

"Just allow the fizz to relax your brain, Millie-girl," said Dr. Marvel.

He'd gulped his sherry.

Dr. Marvel began to recount his version of the tale of the missing SIP. Every so often, he invited me to add my bits.

When we got to the part about the twins' snooping, the wild chase by Professor Grimm's visitor, and the twins stumbling into Dr. Marvel's living room, I remembered the secrecy bands.

"Dr. M, is it time to remove those?" I pointed to the twin's wrists.

"Ah-ha!" exclaimed Dr. Marvel.

Reuben coughed.

Robert looked embarrassed.

Dr. Marvel extracted a small flat, silver container from his pants pocket. He flipped the lid open and pulled out what looked like a Q-tip. He dipped one end of it into a paste-like substance and rubbed it on Robert's secrecy band. It started to smoke.

Robert flinched.

"Steady, boy," said Dr. Marvel. "This won't hurt."

Within seconds, the band snapped open. Dr. Marvel repeated the same procedure with Reuben.

"How did you boys end up as guinea pigs, anyway?" I asked. "Didn't the hypnosis …" My voice trailed off.

Robert laughed. "Ask him." He elbowed his brother.

Reuben shrugged. "Sorry Dr. Marvel, neither the bands nor the hypnosis worked. We just pretended because we didn't want to be left out."

Dr. Marvel opened and shut his mouth.

Poor D. M, I thought, *a failed invention has left him speechless.*

"So how did you two end two end up here?" I repeated.

"Robert and I thought we had a good plan when we decided to check out the Professor's house—" said Reuben.

"—we were crouched outside his back door when it suddenly flung open," said Robert, his words pouring out in a torrent. "At the same time, someone grabbed us by the scruff. The professor had snuck up behind us."

"It was Mr. Ihaka … er … Saja. He hauled us into the kitchen," said Reuben. "Boy, was he mad! He wouldn't let us leave and he didn't want to hear our excuses."

"He made Professor Grimm slap packaging tape across our mouths and bound our ankles and wrists, too," said Robert.

"Saja said we were about to undergo a life-changing operation," said Rueben.

By the time all our stories were recounted, it was well after midnight. We were all so adrenalin-pumped.

I realized there was no way my dad could report this story to the newspapers or the cops. Nobody would believe any of it, especially since there was no longer any concrete evidence.

The SIP and the aliens were well on their way back to planet Zorb.

I remembered my nametag and pulled it from my pocket. I pinned it to my sweater.

"So this young lady from …" Harry Ihaka squinted at my nametag "… Shoestring Detective Agency … Mitch Jones, P dot I dot?" he chuckled. "PI! Ah, so you are!" He cleared his throat. "If young detective Jones hadn't persisted with her attempts to prove she was as good as her father, we wouldn't have prevented a catastrophe on planet Zorb, and that nasty Saja might have been dissecting me by now."

I smiled. "I can't take all the credit, Mr. Ihaka. Dr. Marvel and my Teddy helped me investigate this case."

"Your Teddy?" chorused several voices.

"Yep! My teddy bear. He's clever, you know. He's here somewhere. I left him in my detective bag."

"Was that your infernal bag sitting outside the back door?" said Dr. Marvel.

"Ah, yes." I stuck my index finger in the air as I had seen him do so often. "That's the one."

"That confounded obstacle sent me flying into the kitchen door like a human cannonball," said Dr. Marvel. "I could have cracked my cranium. I sure don't want to end up more bonkers now, do I?"

The twins and I laughed.

"Sorry, Dr. M, I'd better go get it," I said.

"It's not where you left it, I'm afraid." Dr. Marvel scratched his chin. "I used it for a football. It's probably still rocketing into space, I should imagine." He laughed, and so did the others.

"Ouch! Poor Teddy! How do I get him back?"

Mr. Ihaka cleared his throat. "If it's all right with you lot, I think detective Michelle Jones deserves a free year's pass to Te Papa for her bravery." He raised his glass.

"Here, here! To Michelle," they all agreed.

I cleared my throat. "It's Mitch Jones, PI, remember?" I said.

"When I found the lock to my desk broken, I knew you were up to something, Michelle," said Dad. "I was mad, but I had to get on with the case. I didn't think you could outsmart me like this, though. Well, I guess I owe you an apology. But how did you get into my office?"

I swallowed.

"My skeleton key is where you can't find it … unless … did you … you didn't!"

I wrapped my arms around his waist. "I love you, Dad. Sorry I disobeyed you, but—"

"But your days as an unqualified detective are over, young lady," he interrupted. "Finish your education, then we'll discuss your career options."

I would have argued with Dad, but Teddy was yakking in my head.

"Yo, Mitch Jones PI, that was some fireworks display leaving Grimm's roof … and you never did tell Boraz what "crap" is. And one more thing, please get me down from this stupid Ngaio tree. I don't like heights."

"Teddy's stuck in a Ngaio tree, Dad. We have to rescue him."

Everyone laughed and shook their heads.

"At least he's still safe on good old planet Earth," said Dr. Marvel.

For once, I thought, *Dr. M made perfect sense!*

GLOSSARY

Cabbage tree	A palm-tree-like shrub, native to New Zealand
Karaka	A native tree of New Zealand
Morepork	An owl-like bird, native to New Zealand.
Maori	First settlers of New Zealand
Ngaio	A native tree of New Zealand
Papatoetoe	A small town in New Zealand
Rimu	A native tree of New Zealand
Seatoun	A suburb of Wellington, New Zealand
Silver Fern	Native plant of New Zealand
Tea	In New Zealand, often refers to dinner.
Te Papa	New Zealand's National Museum
Wood pigeon	A large pigeon, native to New Zealand

Caged
Where Most Husbands Should Be ... for a While!

H. Lena Jones

Synopsis

Adamos, a stubborn and inconsiderate husband, determined to break his wife's resolve and self-confidence, decides to leave her. But the tables are turned when he is miraculously transformed into a rabbit and returned to his unsuspecting wife, Eva, to be cared for. He is able to communicate with his sister-in-law (whom he detests), but he is unable to communicate with Eva, although he can understand everything she says.

Trapped in the body of the rabbit, Adamos is forced to listen to Eva's complaints about his rotten treatment of her. He sees the error of his ways and is desperate to reform. When he hears that Eva intends to have him neutered and saddled with a rabbit mate, he is deeply concerned. When Eva declares that she will find herself a new husband, Adamos is livid. He must escape, find the source that transformed him, and beg for the return of his manhood.

Trapped on Planet Liska

H. Lena Jones

Synopsis

Twelve-year-old Leslie Lewis is quarantined with chicken pox. For two consecutive nights, she has a vivid dream about a young boy who is being bullied by classmates. Just as Leslie is about to intervene, she awakes. This annoys her, so she makes a wish to remain in the dream, long enough to help the boy.

Leslie's wish is granted, but she is too late to save the boy; instead, she becomes the bullies' new target. Now she wants out of her dream-world, but finds it impossible to wake up. She is trapped!

Leslie's guardian angel, Zar, materializes in a most unusual manner. He makes a deal with her—the sooner she performs the task of ridding her class of bullying, the sooner she will be able to escape from her dream.

Leslie accepts, but reforming the bullies is no easy task, even with Zar's help.

THE CASE OF THE MISSING SIP

SYNOPSIS

When twelve year-old Michelle Jones is forbidden from helping her dad with his top-secret assignment about a robbery at Te Papa museum in New Zealand, she decides to "go underground" as Mitch Jones, P.I.

Mitch soon discovers that THE CASE OF The MISSING SIP is not an ordinary one. Unexpectedly, she is contacted by aliens from planet Zorb. They need her to reprogram their S1M1 unit, which contains vital information for the survival of their race. If the S1M1 is discovered by their deadly enemy, Saja, he will destroy its sensitive database.

Mitch uncovers information about a stolen Superior Intelligence Protector, as reported by her father's client, the head of security at Te Papa. Now, she has a dilemma. Should she help her dad or her alien friends?

With the help of Dr. Marvel, a nutty retired scientist who the aliens have mysteriously selected as her partner, she somehow manages to keep one step ahead of her father.

Through her determination to prove herself to her dad, while also helping her alien clients, the young PI relentlessly pursues her case to a dramatic conclusion.

978-0-595-41723-0
0-595-41723-X

Printed in the United States
73637LV00003B/180

9 780595 417230